The By Mistake Guide to Norfolk

Demon Dogs, Dragons and Ducks

by J

Go to www.bymistakeguide.co.uk for lots of information on how to follow in Jim's footsteps!

First published in England 2012, Black Dog Books,
104 Trinity Street, Norwich, Norfolk, NR2 2BJ,
www.blackdogbooks.co.uk

Text & illustrations © Caroline Davison
Cover illustration by Claire Kidman

A CIP record of this book is available from the British Library.

ISBN 978-0-9565672-4-6

Printed in Great Britain by HSW Print, South Wales

To Eliot *HAPPY *
from Jim ☺ BIRTHDAY!
+ Caroline

For George

With thanks to Ms Dismore, the staff and
the students of Avenue Junior School, Norwich
for their brilliant feedback!

JANUARY

On the way back from the shops today my big sister, Hannah, announced that she's starting a diary this year because she knows that she's going to be a famous writer when she's older. She said it will be 'amusing', after she's dead, for people to read about her day-to-day life and see how 'brilliant' she was when she was young.

I said it would be 'amusing' after she's dead, full stop. But that was only because she kept hitting me on the head with the diary she'd bought and it's got really sharp corners. Then Mum told me off for wishing my own sister was dead, and Hannah looked all upset like she does when she wants to get me into trouble. And Dad said that if I didn't say sorry we wouldn't go to the beach tomorrow.

1

I said who in their right minds would want to go to the beach in January anyway? It's freezing at the moment, snow and stuff. Then my little sister, Lil, started shouting that we were going to see the seal babies and if I didn't say sorry she'd kick my shin. And then she kicked my shin before I could even start to say 'Noooooooo!' She's only small but she's quick. And anyway, I was trapped in the middle of the back seat with no chance of escape.

HELP!

So I'm writing this with a sore head and a bruised shin, AND I had to say sorry. But it's OK because when Hannah wasn't looking I stole her diary. She's been looking for it all evening, HA HA! And now I'M writing in it because if anyone's going to be a genius around here, it's ME!!!!

***

So today we went to the beach. It was really, REALLY cold, and somehow I got stuck in the middle of the back seat again. It's not fair. Hannah reads all the time when we're in the car and she says she has to be near an open window otherwise she'll be sick in my lap. And Lil says she's too scared to sit in the middle with no seat in front of her. If I make her sit there, she screams every time a lorry or something comes towards us. Her screams clean your ears out and everybody gets at me for bullying her.

We drove to a place called Horsey. But really it should be called Sealy, because there weren't any horses there at all, or ponies, or donkeys or even cows a long way off that you might think were horses without your glasses on - but there were loads of seals.

When we got to Horsey Dad said we might visit the wind pump. I said that sounded like something nasty that Lil suffers from after eating baked beans. Lil didn't think that was very funny. Mum didn't think it was funny either and told us that actually wind pumps were small windmills used for pumping water off the

PARDON!

marshes in the old days. I should explain: my Mum is very keen on old things and thinks we are too.

Anyway, the mill wasn't open 'cos it's winter which was annoying. But Dad said we hadn't come to see the mill and he parked by the pub, and dragged us up this long track, with the wind blowing straight off the sea and that was when I wished I hadn't said sorry yesterday, and we could've stayed at home. But then we got to the sand dunes, and walked along them a bit and I could see a pile of rocks lying on the beach in the distance - except they KEPT MOVING!! And it turned out they were seals - loads of them - lolling about on the edge of the sea as if it was all warm and cosy and they were sunbathing. They looked like great big pork sausages with fins and tails.

In amongst the grown ups there were some younger fluffier ones and when Lil saw those she stopped thinking straight and just kept going 'aahhh, sweeeet!' for about the next hour in an annoying way. She prefers animals to people. Hannah lectured us on the difference between common seals, which are grey and aren't common, and grey seals which aren't really grey at all but are brown and grey and white and speckled and are common. Or something like that. The pups looked like very large cuddly toys, with big dark eyes and silly grins on their faces. But the adults were really grumpy and wobbly (why did I think of my Dad then?) and made a whining noise like Lil when she's been told to go to bed.

There were quite a few people there with binoculars and one of them let me have a look through his. He said in the summer the seals often come and look at you if you're swimming in the sea, which I thought would be cool.

That's when we should have maybe stopped talking because then he said 'don't stay too late though or you might meet Black Shuck.' And he laughed hysterically like one of those mad grown ups in Scooby-doo who are supposed to be friendly but turn out to be secretly plotting to destroy the world. I heard myself say 'who's Black Shuck?' and he made a weird face which I think was supposed to be spooky but looked like he was chewing on a lemon, and sort of whispered,

'Black Shuck is the big black dog from hell. He's got fiery red eyes, and anyone unlucky enough to see him is not long for this world. He's been running round Norfolk every night since his two masters were drowned hundreds of years ago. One was buried at King's Lynn, one at Yarmouth. He goes backwards and forwards visiting their graves and brings death to anyone who gets in his way.'

At that point I said maybe he should stop or he might give Lil nightmares.

Afterwards we had lunch in the Nelson's Head pub and I had fun freaking Lil out about how the pub got its name:

1. They stored Nelson's head in a barrel of beer at the back (Dad looked a bit sick at that point - he was drinking a pint of Nelson's Revenge)

OUCH!

2. His head was found on the beach here after the Battle of Trafalgar (Hannah said this was silly because he only ever lost an eye and an arm, not his head. But who's interested in facts?)

WHERE'S MY HEAD GONE?

3. They stuck his head on a spike outside to scare off pirates.

Lil started poking me in the stomach at that point and made me choke on my crisps and then I had an embarrassing 'wind pumping' experience of my own. Oops. I said the dog at the next table did it (a small brown sausage dog - definitely not Black Shuck). Think I got away with it.

Mum drove back, and Dad deafened us all with his snoring. Nelson's revenge or what.

***

Excuse me if my writing is a bit shaky but my fingers are frozen. We've just got back from one of my Mum's mystery tours. Earlier this afternoon she decided we'd been 'moping about indoors' for long enough and that we all needed to get some fresh air. I looked up the meaning of 'to mope' and I think my Mum doesn't know what she was talking about - we weren't 'gloomy' or 'dull' like it said in the dictionary. I was cosy and happy playing on the x-box in my bedroom, Hannah was weirdly cheerful doing her chemistry project, and Lil was in the middle of dressing up as a medieval princess (i.e. wrapped up in a velvet curtain with a cardboard cone on her head). But we had no choice - Mum said she would ban TV for a week if we grumbled.

ME PLAYING X-BOX

It was late afternoon when we arrived at this tiny railway station next to a marsh in the middle of nowhere. No cafe or toilets or anything. Somewhere called Buckenham. And it was actually freezing. I thought maybe my Mum had gone a bit mad. We stood on the platform and she kept saying, 'just wait and see'. I wondered whether she'd been reading too much Harry Potter to Lil, and was expecting some sort of magic train or something. A couple of ordinary ones went past. Mum brought out a flask of cocoa and things looked up a bit.

It was really REALLY cold, and the sun had nearly gone down. And then these black birds started arriving - great long lines of them suddenly appearing out of the sky. I thought they were crows but Hannah put on her 'I'm going to say something really clever now' face and said 'a crow in a crowd is a rook, a rook on its own is a crow'. Luckily Mum translated this for me and said they were rooks.

ROOKS

CROW

They flew towards us and landed in the field and on the telegraph wires behind the station. That went on for about half an hour, long lines of birds flying from all directions, and it was quite cool, but then they stopped coming and I thought that was it, and we could go home.

I seriously thought I had hypothermia by then. And Lil had gone a funny blue colour. She said she was as cold as an icicle on a glacier in the North Pole. I said I was as cold as an icicle on a glacier in the North Pole that was stuck in a sheet of ice, and Hannah said she was as cold as an icicle on a glacier in a sheet of ice in Antarctica where those penguins live. I said aha, I'm as cold as an icicle on a glacier stuck in a sheet of ice in Antarctica

under a penguin's bottom, and Hannah said
that would be quite warm, and I said that
penguins' bottoms were known for being
cold, with all that sitting around in snow
blizzards. She was about to put me right
but luckily just then all the rooks suddenly
lifted up into the sky at the same time
making a huge racket like:

1. a detuned radio through a thousand
   speakers (Mum's idea).
2. gigantic hailstones on a conservatory
   roof (my idea)
3. pebbles being rattled in a tin
   bowl (Hannah's idea)
4. I don't like it, it's too loud, I
   want to get in the car (Lil's idea).

The birds swirled about in a huge black
cloud right over our heads.
We were all looking up
at them and Hannah got
a poo dropped splat! on

OOPS!

SPLAT.

her nose. Justice! I haven't laughed so much for weeks. Or ever, possibly.

There was one thing that was a bit weird. Just before the birds all went up into the sky I heard a dog howling. It sounded like a wolf, and I thought maybe it was the howling that had disturbed the birds. Mum said she didn't hear it, and Lil thumped me and said I was just trying to freak her out. Hannah heard it though. She tried to look all witchy (not difficult) and went:

'WoOoOOoo! Maybe the name of the place should be Black Shuckenham, not Buckenham.' But I couldn't take her seriously with the bird poo still on her nose.

When I got home I looked up Black Shuck on the computer to see if that bloke at Horsey had been making it up -

and he hadn't. There are loads of stories about people seeing a scary giant dog with red eyes that roams the country lanes of Norfolk after dark. The freaky thing is that, if you do see him, something horrible will happen to you - like dying or being given loads of homework. Help!

Hannah came in when I was looking this stuff up and was really annoying about me being a scaredy cat and how 'as a scientist' she doesn't believe in such silly ghost stories. She said smugglers used to make ghost stories up so that local people were too frightened to go out at night. And then the smugglers could get on with their smuggling without being seen. I said she wasn't a smug-gler, she was just SMUG. Ha! But I only thought of it after she'd left the room. That always happens.

Wooooo!

FEBRUARY

Half term hol. Whoopee!

We went to this quite weird place today called Walsingham, full of nuns, and shops full of icons. I didn't know what icons were, but they seem to be pictures of Jesus with lots of gold paint on them, in different sizes. It was quite cool, 'cos one shop sold all those things you see in churches like crosses and huge candles and stuff, and those red and white dress-type things that bishops wear. Lil got really excited but we weren't allowed to try them on.

SPOT THE DIFFERENCE

NUN   PENGUIN

The reason for all the nuns is because some time hundreds of years ago a girl saw a vision of Mary (Jesus's mum). And so ever since then loads of people have gone there hoping they might see her too - which is weird because I reckon 'vision' is just a posh way of saying 'GHOOOST!!'

Anyway, the real point of going there was to see the snowdrops. There's a ruined abbey, where monks used to live and they must have spent most of their time planting snowdrops rather than praying, because the place is covered in them. Maybe planting snowdrops got you out of other nasty tasks?

Monk-in-charge (just leaving the loo the morning after eating bean casserole): *The toilet is in need of a good scrub. Monk 1, could you clean it please?*
Monk 1: *Er, sorry Monk-in-charge, but I've got a heck of a lot of snowdrop planting to do. I'll do it this evening if I have time.*

Monk-in-charge: What about you Monk 2?

Monk 2: Normally, I'd love to. You know I would. It's a privilege to clean up after you, Monk-in-charge. But I'm horribly behind with my snowdrop planting I've only managed one million this week, and my target is three million. I got side-tracked by Monk-second-in-command, who needed his daffodils planting.

Monk-in-charge: Yes, yes, I quite under - stand. What about you, Monk 3?

Monk 3: Oh, what a shame! I'd have loved to, your holiness, but all this awful snowdrop planting means I just don't have the time these days for the jobs I used to love doing, like cleaning loos, scrubbing floors or washing all the monks' clothes. I worked until midnight last night, and was up at dawn, out planting another million snowdrops before breakfast.

Monk-in-charge: Well, I'm sorry to hear that, Monk 3. But of course, though snowdrop planting is a hard and difficult job, someone's gotta do it! I won't keep you any longer. You'd better just show me where the toilet brush is.

The snowdrops do actually look a bit like snow, if you get down close to the ground and let your eyes go out of focus - which I did by mistake at one point when Lil attacked me from behind with a large stick. Apparently she was Robin Hood and I was Friar Tuck. I pointed out that Friar Tuck was on Robin Hood's side, but, as I might have mentioned, she's not good at reasoning. She just hit me a bit harder for talking back.

Luckily it wasn't too far to walk and there was the promise of cake afterwards. Mum bet us £10 we couldn't find a snowdrop with yellow markings instead of green. We should have known it was pretty impossible, 'cos her reward rate is usually £1. We didn't find a yellow snowdrop. Anyway, there's something wrong with the idea of yellow snow.

While we were waiting for our cake to arrive in the cafe afterwards Mum and Dad got fed up with us 'cos we were arguing. Hannah started it because she went to sit on the chair I wanted to sit on, looking out of the window. Everyone knows I always want to sit where I can look out of the window. This is because once when we were on holiday, and I wasn't looking out of the window, the others saw a large white rabbit run past with a hat on, and I missed it (they swear they did, even Mum, so I have to believe them). I don't want to take that chance again.

LIL

So I tried to push Hannah away from the chair - obviously - and while we were fighting, Lil sat there instead. So then we both tried to push her off. Dad got cross and said we couldn't have any cake if we didn't sit down IMMEDIATELY.

HANNAH

Mum tried to calm things down by saying we all had to do a drawing of what we thought the Abbey church would've looked like when it wasn't a ruin - she drew the archway on three different paper napkins and said the person who drew the best one would get a prize. Here are the three draw- ings - no prizes for guessing which is mine.

JIM

Mum did her usual 'fair' thing of giving us each a £1 - she said Lil's was the most artistic, Hannah's was the most historically accurate, and mine was the most, er, imaginative.

Why do I always think the prize is going to be something exciting, like a swiss army knife or an ipod? I fall for it every time.

Afterwards my Dad said that, while we were busy drawing, a bishop in a red dress ran past the window being chased by a big black dog - I THINK he was joking. Hannah must have told him how I was freaked by that dog howling and the Black Shuck story.

Which reminds me. I've decided to start a Black Shuck monitor - before we go out anywhere I'm going to check it out on the web to see if the demon dog might turn up there and I need to be scared. I was pretty relaxed today because I thought probably all those icons and nuns and bishops dresses would keep the scary things away. But it seems you can't be too careful.....

I really don't think it's fair that just because Hannah is obsessed with something that M&D approve of, we ALL have to join in with it. Hannah is obsessed with bird watching so now every weekend we seem to go off into the middle of nowhere to see if we can find purple-eared geese, bright red shanks, spotty-nosed flinks, green-shaggy yodellers, lesser-feathered widgets, tatty-bald buntings, brown-bellied porkers and so on and so on (I think we did see at least one of those today).

ACNE

SPOTTY
NOSED
FLINK

OINK!

BROWN
BELLIED
PORKER

Dad said she'd become a proper twitcher, and I

expected her to thump him or something, because that sounds like an insult. But she was pleased because apparently a twitcher is what you call an obsessive bird-watcher.

But even though they know I'm kind of interested in that Black Shuck story and ghosty-type things they don't take any notice at all, accept to tell me not to be silly, because ghosts don't exist. Well, lots of people on the web disagree with them. For instance, today M&D said we were going to somewhere called Burra (which I found out later is spelt Burgh) Castle where there are lots of birds. So I did a search and found out that the place is stuffed full of ghosts and unexplained shrieking:

TATTY
BALD
BUNTING

BLACK SHUCK MONITOR: The demon dog haunts the castle grounds, his single eye glowing red and yellow (that's a clever trick!).

OTHER SPOOKS: On 11th July old ships can be seen sailing towards Burgh Castle. On 14th September you might see a battle between a pirate ship and two smaller boats. On 27th April you can hear the sounds of clashing swords and Roman and Saxon screaming (!??). On any dark night you might also see a figure falling from the ramparts - better take a torch if it's <u>that</u> dark, or it might be <u>you</u>...

Blimey! It seemed quite a nice place when we were there. Luckily the worst things don't happen in March so I was glad we went today. Even so, I couldn't help feeling a bit worried.

On our way from the car park we passed the church which has a round tower. Mum got us to try and guess why it was round (potential prize: a packet of crisps from the pub). So we made a list:

1 It was a helter-skelter for monks (on their days off from snowdrop planting).
2 It was a dodgy exhaust pipe which dropped off a giant UFO OR
3 the whole world is actually a space ship and the tower is the world's exhaust pipe.
4 It started off as a chimney and the rest of the building is underground.
5 It started off as an underground well and the earth has been dug away.
6 In the old days people thought round was cool and square wasn't.
7 In the old days people thought demons hid in corners so they banned them.
8 Corners get dusty - the vicar's cleaner didn't like them.

9 It's the fossilised tentacle of a giant prehistoric octopus.
10 It's a giant mammoth's fos-silized trunk.

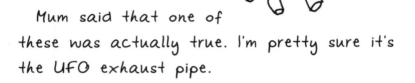

Mum said that one of these was actually true. I'm pretty sure it's the UFO exhaust pipe.

Then we walked across the field to this really HUGE ruined Roman fort. Hannah Smarty-pants pointed out that 'burgh' means 'castle' in Ye Olde English. So when you say 'I'm going to visit Burgh Castle Fort' it's like saying 'I'm going to visit Castle Castle Castle'. Which is silly.

Did the people living there think that if they said everything three times we'd under-stand it better? Did they think that if they said everything three times we'd understand it better??!! I said:

DID THEY THINK IF THEY SAID
EVERYTHING THREE TIMES
WE'D UNDERSTAND
IT BET-
TER??!!

Well, it didn't
work.

<u>OR</u>

  They might've
had to say everything
three times because they were deafened by
the screaming of ghosts. There was a horrible battle here and lots of people were
thrown from the walls of the fort down
into the river and that's why you can hear
ghostly Roman and Saxon shrieking. But I'm
not sure what that would sound like - do
people shriek differently in different lan-
guages?. Imagine....

......A Saxon climbs up the wall of the battlements and comes face to face with a Roman. The Roman hits him on the head but the Saxon manages to whack the Roman with his sword:

SAXON: AACH!

ROMAN: OOPHIO!!

The Saxon swipes with his sword again and chops off the head of the Roman, but not before the Roman has pushed the Saxon off the battlement to fall to his death in the river far below:

30

ROMAN: ARRGH!O!
SAXON: HA! UH? AAAAAACCCC#######hhhhh!!!
SPLOSH!!!........

We had a picnic leaning against those huge walls - which wasn't very comfortable actually as flints are very sharp.

After that Hannah wanted to go and look at the birds so we went down to the path below the fort which leads to the main river bank. As we were walking past the tall reeds a really weird screamy noise came from inside the middle of them. We all stopped in our tracks.

I thought 'AARGH!! SCARY GHOST SAXON MONSTER!!' and then 'Pull yourself together, Jim, no-one else is running' all in about a tenth of a second, which, as I pointed out at the time, goes to show how we have evolved from monkeys into intelligent human beings.

SPOT THE DIFFERENCE

Hannah seemed to think this was hilarious, for some reason. And I thought she was good at science.

We stood listening for a bit but the noise didn't happen again. I said it had sounded like Lil when she's seen a spider in the bath - a kind of high pitched 'Ueeeeeeeeeeeeeeeeee!!! Ueeeeeeeeeeeeeee!!! Ueeeeeeeeeeeeeeeeeee!!!'

Hannah said it was the noise I make when Lil rugby tackles me without warning. Then Lil rugby tackled me without warning and I think the noise I made was more like 'ooooophhhherrrrrrrraarrrghoooowwwwwwww!!!' so Hannah was wrong and looked very silly.

Mum said the noise was more like an angry pig (why did I think of Dad then?). I don't actually know what an angry pig

sounds like but anyway we didn't think
there could be a pig hiding in the reeds.
So I'm pretty sure it
actually was a SCARY
GHOST SAXON
MONSTER!!!!!!
AARGGHH!!!

Ueeeeee!!

Smarty-pants
Hannah, as usual,
came up with a 'sensible'
answer. One of her twitcher tweeters -
excuse me while I untie the knot in my
tongue - said it was probably a Water
Rail, which is some kind of bird that
creeps around in the reeds and scares people by screaming its head off, just for a
laugh. So that made me think that if in
the old days there were lots of those birds
creeping about in the mist and the gloom
making that funny noise, the locals would
have definitely thought it was SCARY
GHOST SAXON MONSTERS!!!. I mean if

you were an ignorant peasant, you would think that, wouldn't you?

The bird Hannah really wanted to see has got several names - a bit like Burgh Castle Fort. It's called a 'lapwing' and its called Vanellus vanellus (another case of Romans repeating themselves), and it's also called a 'Peewit'. I'm sorry? **Peewit**???

NO ROOM FOR BRAIN

Hannah said it was because of the sound they make, but it's obvious someone made that story up to hide the fact that it's a rude name for a bird with little brain. The kind of insult a Saxon might shout in anger at a Roman: Imagine...

A Roman clonks a Saxon on the head with a large stick and pushes him off the battlements to his certain death.

34

ROMAN: *Takus that-io!!*
SAXON: *AAAACCCC### YOU*
PEEEEEEEEEEEE wiiiit!!!!!
SPLOS#!!!

Me and Lil had a look for stuff left by
the Romans (someone once found a helmet)
or bits of dead Saxon - but no luck. It
was really REALLY windy today and got
a bit cold. So in the end me and Lil and
Mum went to the pub to eat the promised
crisps, and we left Hannah and Dad looking at geese with pink feet on the mud
flats.

Lil said she'd like to buy the
geese slippers. I though
wellies might be more prac-
tical - but as Lil pointed
out, once they were on, how
would the geese get the wellies
off again? It usually takes at
least two grown adults and an

elephant
(if there
happens
to be one
passing by) to
get them off my feet.

And we also decided that the first things the Romans said when they arrived here from nice sunny Italy was probably BBbbrrr! Hence the name: BBbbrrr castle.

***

It's the Easter Hols! Whooppee!

Our cousins Jon (mad in a good way) and George (mental in a good way) and their mum, Aunt Ali, are staying with us. It was Mother's Day today so we had to do what the Mums wanted with no complaining. Lil has been doing the Stone Age at school so our Mum thought it would be a good idea to go to this place called Grimes

Graves. I didn't think it sounded much fun - a kind of grubby churchyard perhaps, but I managed not to say so.

BLACK SHUCK MONITOR: the place we went to is near the Peddars Way, an old Roman Road, which Black Shuck is supposed to run along looking for his master. That's when he's not running round the coast looking for his master. This demon dog is one confused ghost. Someone needs to give him a satnav.

OTHER SPOOKS: Grime's Graves was first called Grim's Graves and Grim was the ancient god of the underworld - so nothing to be scared of, then!

Me, Jon and George went in one car with the Mums. On the way there we went

past a race track and one of us said
something about fast cars but Aunt Ali
thought we said something about vast
scars and then, after we'd laughed at her
for several minutes, we ended up inventing
this game where you have to think of two
words that rhyme with 'fast cars' and then
give a clue to them - like 'Singing a long
time ago' (Past lahs). There were some
others like:

1   The final chocolate bar
2   Infinite universe
3   Posh person
talking about
his most
horrible
twelve months
4   Sailors who climb
up to the look-out (Aunt Ali did
that one and we took ages to
get it)

Then we went through a place called 'Two Mile Bottom - and couldn't help using that as a clue as well...Think about it!

Our Mums didn't think it was funny - but luckily, at that point, we arrived.

0   1   2 miles

It turns out it's not graves at all, but a place where stone age people dug up flints to use for skinning animals and stuff. They dug great big pits using antlers. I thought about how long it takes to dig a hole on the beach with a proper spade and it made me glad I wasn't a stone age boy, even though they were lucky not to have school or sprouts then, and you could throw spears at things and no-one complained - unless you happened to hit them maybe. And even then they would've only said something like 'Ug' which isn't as scary as 'WHAT do you think you're doing!? Stop doing that immediately and go to the head teacher's office!'

Which, you know, a teacher might say, if you were practis- ing with a javelin and it kind of slipped and went a bit near the rest of the class, by mistake, because you were being attacked by a wasp, and it honestly wasn't your fault.

oops!

I mean it could've happened to <u>anyone</u>.

Anyway, at this Grimes Graves place you could go down into one of the mines which was cool. I was the first to climb down the ladder and it was a bit spooky at the

bottom on my own, imagining stone age
people hacking away at the rock, going
'Ug!' at each other, and the god of the
underworld just hiding
around the corner.
All the other mines
were filled up with
rubble which has
sunk down over the
years, so now the
whole place is covered in
little round dips like the
surface of a golf ball. We
had a lot of fun running around
trying to push each other into the

DEADLY PITS OF DOOM!

Mum came out of the info centre and said there was an interesting film about some flint napping and I thought that sounded about as interesting as watching paint dry:

'Welcome to this marvel - lous opportunity to see a stone asleep in its natural habitat!...we must, of course, be very quiet and try not to disturb it...Oh look, the stone's not moving! It's having a well-earned nap...Oh, wait, look!....no, it's still sleeping. And..........it's not moving. It's completely and utterly motionless.....Hang on a minute!................ no, it's still sitting there, not moving. Well, that's fascinating....wait!.........no. Still asleep...And now....back to the studio....'

Anyway it turned out it wasn't about napping, it was about 'knapping' which is

chipping bits off big lumps of flint to make
smaller bits with sharp edges for arrow
heads and daggers and stuff. After watching the film Lil spent a long time looking
for bits of flint to tie to the end of a
stick to make a stone age arrow. I think
she'd got a bit tired of being pushed into
the

DEADLY PITS OF DOOM!

She had that look on her face that means
trouble. I felt a bit like mammoths must
have felt just before they went extinct.
Slightly nervous.

After that we went to a nature reserve
nearby. It was used as an aerodrome in

the second world war and there are still
some old buildings left over from them. So
we had some more fun running around
playing the

DEADLY HUTS OF DOOM!

There were zillions of rabbits hopping
around on the grass there. I've never seen
so many. Hannah said it was because rabbits were brought here by the Normans to
be kept for eating, the same as pigs or
sheep, but then they escaped into the wild.
I said, oh yeah, that's right, and the poor
little bunny-wunnies were cold and the big
Normans had to make nice cosy burrows
for them. And Hannah looked really

shocked and said 'yeah, that's right. How did you know?'

So I looked all clever and said 'Aha, that would be telling, smarty-pants.' But actually I had no idea what she was going on about. Then I overheard Mum telling Aunty Ali that the Normans did bring rabbits here and the soppy creatures really didn't know how to dig burrows properly. The foxes must have been thrilled - the first fast food take-away for wild animals: 'Wow! Forget those tough old sheep with the wool that sticks in your teeth. These new bite-sized French furry snacks are well tasty, and sooooo convenient!'

SWEEET LEETLE BUNNY!

We had a picnic sitting in the bracken and saw a yellow butterfly and some lambs bouncing around - that means it really is Spring. It was warm and I'd had at least three bacon sandwiches and couldn't help shutting my eyes for about two seconds. Bad mistake. Lil saw her chance and the next things I knew I had fistfuls of dry scratchy bracken stuffed up my t-shirt. It was NOT funny. I can still feel little bits in places you don't want to know about.

APRIL

It was actually hot today!! We went to Holt in the morning - M&D like the shops there for some reason - all posh clothes and old furniture. We had a good lunch - really posh bacon sandwiches! And we went into the book shop, and Mum bought me a book about Norfolk ghosts because she'll buy me anything if she thinks it'll make me read.

I wanted to find out more about Black Shuck and there was a whole chapter on him. It says that the scary black dog idea comes from the Celts who believed in monster dogs that were spirits of the underworld looking for human souls to devour. That made me feel a bit queasy.

HELP!

It sounds kind of painful. I have this nasty feeling, every time we go out, that there might be a scary black dog waiting round the corner, ready to jump on me. So I wasn't keen to go out into the countryside but no-one takes any notice of me. We went to a place called Baconsthorpe - cool name, though if I lived there I'd probably want to eat bacon sandwiches the whole time. There's a ruined castle which we had a good look round.

BLACK SHUCK MONITOR: No sightings!
OTHER SPOOKS: a ghostly soldier stands on the walls of the castle and throws stones into the moat. Luckily I didn't know this until we got home when I looked the castle up on the computer. Eek! Now I think about it we <u>did</u> hear some splashes - I thought it was the ducks...

DUCK!

Mum said the family who built the castle got really rich very quickly and then spent it all on stuff - probably large amounts of bacon - until in the end they were so poor they had to knock down most of the castle and sell the bits off to be used in other buildings. I thought that was a good money-making idea and suggested we knock down the back extension to our house which has got the bathroom and Hannah's bedroom in it. I'm sure we could manage without them.

There's a big green pond in one corner which looked stagnant and was a bit smelly. Hannah said in her teacher's voice that this was part of another money-spinning venture, to make woollen cloth. Apparently, people used to fill the tank with wee - yes, it _is_ disgusting - and then walk on the wool in their bare feet to make it

49

soft – yes, it is really REALLY disgusting. That's what the man on the audio guide said: the wool was 'trodden under foot in urine' as if it's the most normal thing in the world! You wonder how they found out it made wool soft. Imagine...

Tudor peasant 1: 'I'm bored. What shall we do?'

Tudor peasant 2: 'I don't know. I've got this bit of wool here and I'm dying for a wee.'

Tudor peasant 1: 'Are you thinking what I'm thinking?'

Tudor peasant 2: 'Yes! Quick, let's put the

wool in this large empty pond and I'll wee on it.'

Tudor peasant 1: 'Brilliant idea! And just for fun why don't we take our socks off and jump around in it?'

Tudor peasant 2: 'Genius! And, Oh my god! this wool feels really soft!'

Tudor peasant 1: 'Best fun I've had since that swim in the moat...'

Which actually would also have been disgusting, because I found out that the tunnels in the walls that me and Lil had been crawling through were the old sewers where people used to poo, straight down into the moat. Urrgh! The moat must have been really stinky, and a bit lumpy, even though the pictures on the info boards make it look all blue and pretty, and not like an unflushed toilet. DIS. GUST. ING!!

51

It's quite OK now though with lots of birds swimming around on it, and I managed to eat the cake Mum had brought us from the shop in Holt without thinking too much about toilets. We sat leaning against the wall, with the sun shining on us and it was hot like summer. Nice.

When we got home I read the book about ghost stories and stuff. It says that in 1577 the devil appeared as a giant black dog in the churches at Bungay and Blythburgh - which are in Suffolk so the demon dog got around a bit. He actually killed some people, and at Blythburgh there are scorch marks on the door made by his claws. I emailed my mate Will who lives near there, to see if he knew about it. He said he'd get his parent's to take him on a visit.

SCREECH!

Dad is very keen on mills and old machinery of any sort but he's especially mad about watermills. So in the summer he sometimes helps run an old water mill at Gunton, and we have to go too. They open the sluice and all this water from the lake rushes in and makes the waterwheel turn - and then that makes a huge upright saw work inside the mill. It cuts through whole trees like they were butter and it's really noisy. Mum finds it a bit worrying - she says it makes her fingers nervous - so she tends to sit by the lake and look at the ducks while we're there.

The building is thatched and looks like the kind of place a witch might live in - and the machinery inside looks like her evil torture equipment. That's what Lil thinks, anyway. It's the kind of place where James Bond would be strapped to the tree trunk in chains, edging ever nearer to the lethal sharp saw which threatens to slice him in a VERY uncomfortable place, and the evil Dr No would be laughing:

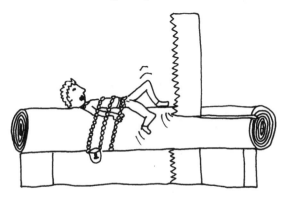

'Mwahaha! And so Mr Bond, we meet again - and for the last time!! Mwahaha! Before you die your most horrible death, I must just tell you all the details of my cunning plan so that when at the very last moment, you pull free from those enormous padlocks, use your biro to jam the savage circular saw, and leap onto a handy motorbike which I have carelessly left there for your escape – I will have told you all the information you need to prevent me, yet again, from destroying the WORLD!!! MWahaha!!!'

Will he never learn?

We watched a whole tree trunk being sawn in two, and then went outside. The mill is in the grounds of a huge house with a park full of deer which were wandering about on the other side of the lake. Then Mum said she was going to look at the church. My face was like:

Then she said, 'Oh, don't be like that. It's interesting. It looks like a Roman Temple.' My face was like:

Then she said, 'If you walk there with me I'll let you have one of your bacon sand-wiches.' My face was like:

My Mum knows me too well.

Lil said I would probably swim across a shark-infested river if there was a bacon sandwich on the other side, and Hannah said she didn't think sharks lived in rivers, but she thought I would probably have a go at swimming across a river full of piranhas, and I said that they were both being very silly and that, in fact, I would swim across a river of boiling lava full of piranhas and sharks if there was a bacon sandwich on the other side, and as long as I could be sure it hadn't got burnt by the lava - I don't like my bacon over-cooked.

Hannah pointed out that if there were sharks and piranhas swimming in the lava they would be burnt to a frazzle, and that it wouldn't matter too much if the bacon sandwich was a bit over-cooked, as I'd be burnt to a frazzle as well. Which is boring but true - she is always sooo boring but sooo right. So I asked her: 'what is a frazzle?' That shut her up for a bit.

BLACK SHUCK MONITOR   No sightings!
OTHER SPOOKS: A female ghost can be heard to scream just before any of the family living at the Hall are about to die. She can sometimes be seen gliding across the park.

We walked to the church along the lane that runs through the haunted park but didn't see any floating ladies. We had to go passed several 'Strictly private' signs, which Lil really didn't like. She said if it had just said 'private' she wouldn't have

felt so worried but she was scared of the
'strict' word – it sounded as if her scary
piano teacher was going to jump out of
the bushes and speak very sternly to her
about naughty little girls who don't practise their scales and don't keep their nails
clean (she knows what it's like). But Mum
said it was ok because peasants like us
are still allowed to visit the church. So as
we walked past the front of the big house
we pretended we were disgusting filthy
ancient Britons on our way to visit a
Roman temple and Lil forgot to worry.
Pretending to be a disgusting filthy ancient
Briton comes naturally to her.

SPOT THE DIFFERENCE

PEASANT

PHEASANT

Mum was
telling the
truth
though – the
church did look
like a temple, and
nothing like the usual

churches we get dragged to. It's quite sinister with lots of blocked windows and blank walls, a bit like a prison. While the others had a look inside I sat on the bench with the sun on my face and ate my bacon sandwich. Being a disgusting filthy modern Briton felt GOOD!

When we got back to the mill Dad said he'd only cut off two fingers on his right hand and three on his left so it had been a good day. He is soooooooooo funny. Not.

This evening Will emailed me to say he'd been to Blythburgh church and it was true - the scorch marks of the Hell Hound <u>are</u> there. 'Sensible' people say it was a massive storm that did all the damage. But how come people in two churches agreed that they'd all seen the Black Dog? And what about those marks? Spooky.

Blickling today. We often go there because the park's free and there's a cafe (mum likes), and a pub (dad likes), and a second hand book shop (Hannah likes), and a shop (Lil likes). I like the trees. There are some trees there that are so big and fat you can get two or three people in them like a fortress, and chuck stuff at each other (depending on the time of year, you can use pine cones, snow, leaves, bits of old sandwich...).

OK! YOU WIN!

We went because the bluebells are flowering. Loads of people were taking photos because there are quite a lot of bluebells. They are actually purple of course but no one seems to want to talk about

that. They should be called purple-petals.
Hannah said that was a stupid idea, and
wouldn't be nearly as good a name for
fitting into poetry and stuff. So I reminded
her of how she usually goes on about the
importance of FACTS, and continued to
call them purple-petals for the rest of
the day. It's funny
watching her face go
red, and the steam
coming out of her ears.

I also wrote a poem to show her how
wrong she is:

How sweet to see the wood in spring,
With nodding Purple-petals,
And listen to Deep Purple songs,
THE sound of heavy metal.

The thing I don't like is the pyramid.
Yes, that's what I said. A PYRAMID. What
is it doing there?? It's all black and
gloomy, and there's a funny feeling about

it, as if it might be an alien spaceship with some sort of evil energy force field around it. There are openings into it on two opposite sides but you can't see much - it just looks dark and spooky. PLUS there's a scary statue of a snarling black dog on one side. Which reminds me:

BLACK SHUCK MONITOR: Help! A really scary story about an evil past owner of the hall who appears as a devilish black dog and drives everybody mad. Is that what the statue is of? Plus some more recent reports of sightings on the lanes nearby...

OTHER SPOOKS: :Tons
of them. Including Ann
Boleyn, holding her head.
~~EE~~eeekkkk!!!

Knowing all that spooky
stuff, I felt a bit nervous
about the pyramid. As we
were walking past it - in a
calm but brisk manner- there was
this terrifying wolf howl that echoed out
from inside it, and I quickly clutched at Lil
- to protect her from whatever it was.
And then there was this horrible echoing
cackle, and we realised it was either a) a
witch or b) Hannah or c) both

It was actually c) - my horrible big
witch-sister who was standing by the open-
ing on the other side of the pyramid and
howling through it. Luckily, the echo dis-
guised some of the words I shouted back
at her from our side. I could see her

laughing at me through the opposite window, but then she suddenly disappeared. It turned out that deadly secret agent Lil had sneaked round and taken her down. Ha! Her talent for violence has its uses sometimes.

It was about then that M&D noticed we weren't walking behind them anymore and they came back and told me and Lil off for getting Hannah muddy. Which is so unfair!

After we'd had a picnic, and a cake from the cafe, Mum said she wanted to go and look in the church. She's always dragging us round churches. Most of them are pretty dull, but sometimes there are some interesting bits like skulls and skeletons and stuff. And it's spooky to think how many dead bodies there are just under your feet. We worked out that if most graveyards have been used for over a thousand years,

and even if only one person a year was buried there....it's a lot of skeletons. And probably there was always more than just one a year. People used to die a lot in the old days.

We looked as usual at the gravestones to see if we could find any funny names e.g Ramsbottom, Pratt, Sillybum (I'm still looking for that one), or sad stories to make Mum cry - like a whole family dying of a disease in one month. That really gets her going. There was one today about an only son dying from some disease he caught fighting in World War I. There was definitely a teardrop in Mum's eye over that one.

The thing that was quite interesting at this church was a huge sculpture inside, of an enormous man lying on a slab of marble, and at each end are MASSIVE scary stone angels with dead eyes like  zombies. I didn't like to turn my back on them. You could imagine one creeping up on you when you weren't looking. You might hear a scraping noise as its stone feet slide across the floor, you start to turn your head, but it's too late, there's a sudden coldness that makes you shiver, an iron-grip upon your shoulder, a terrifying scream.....AARRGHHHH!!!!

Anyway, Lil said she thought it would be weird to come into the church everyday and see a life-size model of your dead husband and that she wouldn't like it. Hannah thought it was terribly romantic. Mum said she thought it was a waste of money and she wouldn't want to be remembered like that. Dad looked relieved and said that was just as well, as he thought he had about enough money saved up for a bunch of flowers from the garage for her grave, and a couple of packets of crisps for after the funeral. Mum didn't think that was funny. We went home after that.

***

When my Mum said we were going to Happisburgh I though it was some kind of funny fast food outlet, and I wondered if we'd be allowed a milkshake and chips. But my Dad said, don't be silly, it's pronounced Haisbrer, NOT Happy's burga.

There are lots of village names in Norfolk which are said in one way, and spelt in another. We thought of quite a few while we were in the car like Costessey which is actually Cossy, and Wymondham which is Windum. I could go on – Dad certainly did, at ENORMOUS length.

We thought these funny names might have happened because:

The sign-maker allowed his cat to walk on the keyboard while he was typing out the name

OR

Norfolk people ate a lot of sugar in the past – they grow a lot of sugarbeet here – and it rotted their teeth so they couldn't speak properly. Imagine trying to say Wymondham without teeth – it would be Winnmmum, wouldn't it?

WINNMMUM

The reason we went to 'Haisbruh' was because the Lighthouse was open. M&D

thought we'd actually enjoy being scared out our wits climbing up a narrow spiralling staircase with a huge drop down on to a concrete floor (actually it was cool). It turned out that Lil was too short to go up - you have to be over a metre tall and even when she stood on tip-toes and hoped no-one would notice she was still only 98cms. It's amazing how such a small person can be so VERY ANGRY!! The man measuring her looked quite scared.

LIL
VERY
ANGRY

In the end, Hannah said she'd stay at the bottom with her - M&D thought she was being kind but basically she's too lazy to climb up 96 stairs.

Anyway, you have to go up this very tall spiral staircase with just a thin little hand-rail thingy between you and certain death. My Mum was really nervous and kept

saying, 'Oh, be careful, stay close to the
wall, don't lean on the handrail, don't look
down, keep an eye on your feet, don't talk,
concentrate' etc etc - she
seemed to think I might
want to throw myself off
and die a grizzly death just
to annoy her and create
extra work for the cleaners.
She is soooo embarrassing.

At the top there's this circular glass
room full of prisms which reflect the light
of one ordinary little light bulb right out
to sea. I took the opportunity to have a
good look up and down the coast for signs
of large black dogs but 'the coast was
clear'. I just happened to ask the lighthouse man whether he'd ever seen any
spooky dog-type creatures from up in the
lighthouse and he went into a great long
talk about how everyone knew that Black
Shuck roamed the coast there, and 'death

had never been far away in the old days when ships were always being wrecked on the shore'.

I think he must have been related to that bloke at Horsey 'cos he made the same kind of weird face when he was telling me all this. He said he'd never seen the dog and he reckoned the flashing light from the lighthouse had scared him away. But then he

HORSEY
MAN

HAPPISBURGH
MAN

started going on about other spooky things.

QUESTION: Why do grown-ups think it's funny to freak out young defenceless children?

Anyway I already knew about the ghost because I'd done my research:

BLACK SHUCK MONITOR: no very serious sightings but it's on the coast where the black dog roams at night...

OTHER SPOOKS: In 1765 pools of blood were found on the beach but no body was found. A few months later men saw a strange figure in the street dressed in sailors clothes - but with no legs and its head dangling backwards. Uurrgh!

The bloke in the lighthouse said that in the old days people would hear the ghost groaning up from the well before storms started. And then he told M&D they should take me to see the mass grave of drowned sailors in the churchyard...

So where did M&D think it would be a good place to eat lunch?

a) on the nice sandy beach
b) in the nice cosy pub
c) on the mound marking a mass grave.
You guessed it ('c' of course).

There was a shipwreck in 1801 (there's a stone there that you can read while trying to eat your bacon sandwich without feeling sick). 400 men were drowned, and 119 eventually got washed up on the shore there. The local people carted them up to the churchyard and chucked them in a big hole, and then covered them up with earth - making the little hill we were sitting on. Nice.

And I wasn't that desperate afterwards to go down onto the beach where the bodies got washed up. Bits might have got left behind. But we did anyway. No one takes any notice of what I think.

The cliff there is collapsing into the sea so people's houses are falling over the edge.

Some people already have to live in cara-
vans because their houses have gone. It
looked scary. In fact I was feeling pretty
exhausted by all the scariness at that
point.

Hannah actually told us something quite interesting that she'd
read in the church. Apparently

LIL'S

thousands and thousands of years ago the
River Thames used to flow out to sea here
instead of near London. And because now
the cliffs are all collapsing it's uncovered
some bits of sharpened flint which prove
that people lived here 800,000 years ago.
That is a lot.

It got me thinking, because
Hannah said there were all
kinds of scary animals here like
hyenas, and sabre-toothed tigers

HANNAH'S

at the same time. We did myths
at school and Myth Braithwaite - sorry I

MINE ¹⁰⁄₁₀

mean Miss Braithwaite - said that myths are sometimes based on a tiny bit of truth which got changed over a long time into a fairy story. So maybe the story-teller started off talking about real-life dangerous animals, and it's got changed over all those years into Black Shuck? I'd feel less nervous if that were true.

The beach was ok in the end - we had a sand castle competition which obviously I won. You have to feel a bit sorry for Mum and her pathetic effort.

MUM'S

We did find a bit of abandoned leg - but it was from a careless crab. Quite useful as a flagpole.

oi!

After we'd had a paddle (V.COLD!!) we went to the pub. And that was when I really began to think I'd gone to sleep and was having a nightmare because there, on the wall, as I walked in through the door, were some pictures of Black Shuck. Great big wolf-like dogs, snarling at me, with eyes shining like lamps. I got that funny feeling they talk about in books when the hairs stand up on the back of your neck.

We sat right next to the pictures and my heartless Dad said 'oh look Jim. Some stuff about that shaggy dog story.' As if I hadn't noticed. Anyway, it turns out that Conan Doyle, the man who invented Sherlock Holmes, stayed here once and wrote one of his stories (about dancing men - must have been frightening if they danced anything like my Dad). And he wrote another story called 'The Hound of the Baskervilles' all about demon dogs, based on stories he was told in Norfolk about Black Shuck!!! I tell you, that dog is on my trail.

So on the way back in the car I was thinking that people from Happisburgh probably called it Haisbruh because they never had time to stop and say the whole word - they were either being chased by a hyena or a Sabre-toothed tiger, or the Hell Hound, or a legless ghost, or possibly running away from collapsing cliffs or from the stench of rotting sailors washed up on the beach. Imagine...

WHAT'S THIS PLACE CALLED?

HAAISBRAAARSHH!!!

***

Half-term hols. Whoopee!

My mum likes gardens and all that, so she quite often makes us go to posh houses and stuff where they have flowers all tidy in borders and you have to be quiet and sensible otherwise people look at you all grumpy - which is boring. But Sheringham Park, where we went today, is better. It's this huge area completely covered in big bushes of rhododendrons like a jungle. I think some of the bushes are over a hundred years old or medieval or something, and they look all gnarled and ancient like in Lord of the Rings.

You can go down tunnels in amongst the branches and explore. M&D found it really hard to keep up with us 'cos they're too tall and old and not very good at bending anymore.

BLACK SHUCK MONITOR: A black dog known as Shock comes out of the sea and runs up the hills. The dog is headless, with a white cloth covering the stump. Scary, <u>yes</u>, but it's not in Sheringham Park.

OTHER SPOOKS: Quite a few, but in Sheringham town. So the park is safe. Or so I thought...

?

BOING!

I told Lil that a strange 'yeti' type animal had been spotted here several times, and it was thought that it was some kind of prehistoric creature which had got trapped after the ice age - a bit like the Loch Ness monster - and still survives all alone on the Sheringham hills. That's why the hill nearby is called Beast On Bump (I know it's spelt Beeston Bump - but she's not very good at spelling yet). This beast is known to live on a diet of rhododendron flowers and pine cones, and probably lives in extremely well hidden underground burrows.

Lil tried to pretend she didn't believe me but she did. It added a bit of excitement to the exploring - for once she didn't keep attacking me with a stick, and she was very quiet and let me lead the way. My rightful position, at last!

But then at one point I looked behind me and she'd DISAPPEARED! I called her a few times but she didn't answer and then I heard a rustling in the bushes in front of me, and it was bit dark and difficult to see, but I'm telling you, I did see something run across the path. When I told M&D

later they said it was probably a fox or a deer - but it was darker than that: a black shadow. It couldn't have been Lil or Hannah messing about because I crashed into them as I was running back the other way - to check Lil was OK and everything.

BEHIND YOU!

So that was a bit freaky.

Afterwards we went up this wooden watch tower in the middle of all the rhododendrons - you can look right over the whole lot. It really does look like a jungle from up there. Mum was going on about how beautiful the sea of flowers was, but

I was wondering whether I'd by mistake come up with the real story behind Black Shuck: perhaps he's some kind of primordial beast that had been left over from prehistoric times?

After that we walked down to the open park which was quite a relief - no cover for scary beasts - just a few cows. We climbed up a really steep hill (who said Norfolk is flat??) and then at the top there was another lookout tower and you could see the steam train from Sheringham puffing along the coast. We tried to count the steps down from the top of the tower but we all got different answers:

Hannah: 189
Lil: 191
Mum: 190
Me: 4 zillion
(I lost
count half
way down when
I tripped and fell
in a bush);
Dad: 'Oh, sorry I forgot
to count after laughing
so much when Jim fell in the
bush'. (He is very cruel).

Mum said she'd pay one of us a £1 to climb up again and double check. I'm usually pretty keen to earn money but I was too tired and emotional by then. Lil went up and got a different answer for going up (190) and coming down (191). So we gave up at that point and went and had a cup of tea.

***

JUNE

Another day, another Buckenham. You'd think people would have a bit more imagination - we went to one Buckenham to see the rooks in January, but today we visited two more Buckenhams - New and Old. For all I know there's another village in Norfolk called Not-So-Old Buckenham and probably another called Passed-Its-Sell-By-Date-and-Smells-a-Bit Buckenham.

Anyway, it was a sunny day and Mum wanted to see the Green-Winged Orchids. I wasn't even slightly interested in seeing Green-Winged Orchids but no-one takes any notice of me. Have I mentioned that before?

Oh, and actually it was Mum's birthday so we kind of had to do whatever she wanted without complaining. Especially after the exploding birthday cake incident.

KABOOM!

Shh! Don't ask.

We went to New Buckenham first and I think it should be prosecuted under the Trades Descriptions Act because it's not 'New' at all. In fact it's one of the oldest looking villages I've been to. It's got this huge open grassy Common which is where the Green-Winged Orchids grow. They should also be prosecuted under the Trades Description Act. If I said Green-Winged Orchid to you you'd imagine a flower with wings that are green, wouldn't you? Well, I looked at these orchids pretty closely (thanks to another classic Lil rugby tackle) and they didn't have wings, and the wings they didn't have weren't green.

Anyway, Mum got pretty excited about them even though they were pink. And Hannah got pretty excited because she saw newts in the pond. The pond is called Spittle Mere, and makes you wonder whether the people who lived here in the old days were keen footballers...
Anyway, I'm glad I wasn't a newt swimming around in it.

When Mum and Hannah had both calmed down, we walked through the village to get to the castle. On the way we passed a building that looked a bit like a Tudor bus shelter and, inside, there was a wooden pillar holding up the roof and Mum said it was a whipping post. It had metal loops on it at different levels which criminals were chained to and then they were whipped in public in the middle of the village!! Some of those metal loops were pretty low down - about my height. I put my hands in just to see, and Lil immediately started thwacking me on the back with a stick she'd found on the common (I am seriously worried about that girl).

COOL!

And I had this funny moment when suddenly a whole story went through my head, that I was a poor boy in Tudor times, and my mum was ill, and my dad was in prison, and I hadn't eaten for days and - I couldn't help myself - I stole a loaf of bread that was cooling on the window sill of one

of the cottages, it smelt so nice and I was
soooo hungry, and then the woman from
across the road saw me and chased me,
and I dropped that lovely loaf in the mud,
and tried to escape but a man coming the
other way heard the woman shouting and
he grabbed me, and took me to the con-
stable, and they said I would be hanged
but the woman who'd cooked the bread,
and who was kind hearted, said I
should just get a whipping instead
- and I was grateful!

Whoa! That
was weird! I
think it
might've
been the
result of a
major sugar-rush to the brain - well, someone had to hide the exploded cake evi-
dence. Where better than in my stomach?

Or maybe it had something to do with Lil hitting me on the head with the stick?

After M&D had pulled her off me, we went to look at the castle. There's a proper moat there with water in it, and a bridge. And there are supposed to be three tunnels under the castle somewhere which used to lead to three big old houses nearby - but we couldn't find them. By the way:

BLACK SHUCK MONITOR: No sightings. Result!

OTHER SPOOKS: A dark, shadowy ghost walks along Sandy Lane - but only at night and anyway, where is Sandy Lane? Not very scary. Most self-respecting castles have got some sort of ghoul wafting around on the walls screaming and wailing or falling to its death, but not at this one. Obviously there hasn't been enough violent death here (just whipping and spitting).

Lil came quite close to violent death today though. She was being really REALLY annoying. She decided she was the Norman lord who built the place, and I was a peasant (oh how surprising) who needed to be punished for being a peasant

So then I had a GENIUS idea and suggested that if she ran round the earthworks, I'd time how long it took her. She always falls for that one - she thinks she's going to be an olympic sprinter when she grows up. There are these earth banks that go right round the castle in a complete circle, so it's difficult to tell where you started unless you've got a marker. I said I'd be the marker. So she set off, and I counted 'one two, three' until she was far

LIL
VERY
TIRED
HA!

enough round not to be able to hear - and then I hid behind a tree. She'd gone round the whole circuit at least twice before she realised. HA HA! She had a bit less energy for attacking me after that.

We had a picnic sitting in front of the castle and discussed whether the invention of lettuce was a mistake. I made a good speech:

'I, Jim Politician, declare that the abomination known to all as 'lettuce', should never be allowed in civilised society, and in particular should never - I say it again but louder - NEVER! - be allowed in the same room as a bacon sandwich, let alone inside a bacon sandwich, and that, MORE - OVER, those who attempt to feed this vile green cardboard decribed as 'lettuce' to innocent children should be doomed to be fed the stuff for breakfast, lunch and supper for the rest of their years until they are very sorry. And that, MORE - OVER, the said lettuce shall in the future only be used for the feeding of rabbits, tortoises and overweight Dads, and shall never - I say it again but louder - NEVER! - be allowed to terrify the youth of our country in the future, and, MORE - OVER, that I, Jim Politician, shall fight for the right not to be fed this stiff green water described as 'lettuce' so long as I have the breath in my body left to fight.

In fact, ladies and gentleman, I ask you to vote for me and, together, LET US BAN LETTUCE!!'

'Those of you who agree say 'aye'!

Lil: AYE!!
(She's got some sense sometimes)

X   ✓

'Those silly twits of you who don't agree say 'nay'.
Mum & Hannah: NAY!!
(you see, they've eaten so much lettuce they're turning into horses)
Dad: Oi! What do you mean 'over-weight'? That's all muscle, that is!

DREAM   REALITY

So after I'd enjoyed my bacon sandwich with the lettuce taken OUT, we went on to Old Buckenham. Which is old so it wins the prize for being truthful. The reason we went there is because there was a windmill open and Dad loves a windmill. Its the fattest mill in Norfolk. And was one of the most powerful. So a bit like Dad in one way, I'm not saying which. Except, Dad, if you're reading this, it's <u>not</u> muscle- who are you trying to kid? And if you are reading this, well STOP!! This diary is supposed to be private!

MORE CAKE PLEASE

***

Today we went to somewhere just out-side Norwich where there used to be a Roman town called Venta Icenorum (pronounced 'Ika norum' - or, if you get really bored: 'I can ignore 'em'). Lil's doing the Romans at school so M&D thought it would be interesting. For her, maybe. I've done

the Romans about three million times, and
am quite sick of them - I mean what did
they ever do for us? - but we went there-
anyway. What's new.

BLACK SHUCK MONITOR: No official
sightings - but read on...!
OTHER SPOOKS: None. You'd
think there would at least
be a few headless
Roman soldiers, or an
unhappy peasant or
two. Nope. Nil. None.
Nix. Zilch. Zero. Zip.

ZERO

It's one of those places where you have
to use your imagination. That's what my
Dad said anyway. There are huge banks
round the main site and bits of Roman
flint wall. It used to be the biggest town
in this part of the country which is quite
difficult to believe because now it's a
square grassy field in the middle of

95

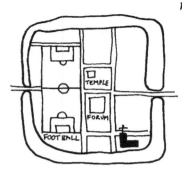

EARLY ROMAN
FOOTBALL
STADIUM

nowhere. The information boards had a photo from the air which showed the lines in the grass where the Roman roads once were. This drawing shows what I think it was but Mum said they didn't play football in those days. I'm not so sure.

Lil had been to the Castle Museum in Norwich with Mum the day before and found out all about who'd lived here. So as usual she wanted to be the Roman warrior in charge and I was supposed to be an Iceni peasant who lived here before the Romans came. Iceni is pronounced 'I seen I' which sounds like something someone thick said to the Romans when they first arrived...

Roman leader: Ahem. I came, I saw, I conquered! As our great leader Julius Caesar once said.

Local country bumpkin: Oh, now that's clever that is. Let's see if I can say that back like you. Now what was it? 'I come, I seen, I fell over'. No, no, no, that weren't it. Let me see. Let's try again.

DER!

Something about conkers, weren't it? ooh, now dont tell me. 'I went, I see, I'm bonkers'. No, it weren't that...

Roman leader: Oh do shut up! Tell me the name of your pathetic little tribe immediately or it will be death by the sword for you!

Local country bumpkin: No, hang on a minute there. What was it again?

Roman leader: Oh really! I don't have time

for this. Tell me the name of your tribe immediately.

Local country bumpkin: Hang about! One more go. 'I seen, I...'

Roman leader: That'll do. 'I seen I'. Write that down somebody. And have one of the gladiators dispose with this idiot, would you? A rusty sword will do.

The leader of the Iceni was a warrior woman called Boudica, pronounced Boo Dicker. Don't laugh. I bet the Romans did, though. It was probably because they were laughing so hard they got defeated by Boudica's army a few times before they started fighting back properly and defeated her.

There's a church in one corner which we went to look at, as always. We couldn't get in at first because it was locked. While Dad went off to get the key we hung about in the porch. On the doorway there was some scratched graffiti of cross-es and what looked a bit like a church from the air (that's what Mum said any-way). Hannah got all snooty about how irresponsible young people are today (except her of course) and then Mum said it was really REALLY old graffiti, like three or four hundred years old, so it was ok.

I said it was probably my duty to scratch 'I WOS 'ERE' on the door post so that future children could see what it was like in the 21st century but my Mum didn't agree. We had quite a long argument about it and she

JIM WAS HERE

started to get cross because she couldn't really say why it was ok for a Tudor boy to do graffiti, but not me. She ended up saying that the Tudor boy probably got whipped for doing it, and that we weren't too far from New Buckenham...Luckily, Dad came back with the key at that point and we went inside.

There was a really faded painting on one of the walls which was supposed to be St Christopher carrying Jesus across a river. Hannah said that there's a painting of him in lots of churches because once you've seen him he'll protect you for the rest of the day. I was really glad about that because - just after - something very scary happened...

Hannah pretended to be the vicar and started lecturing us from the pulpit-thingy about our evil ways and how we would be damned, and stuff like that. (This isn't the scary bit, by the way, though come to think of it, it is pretty terrifying - she'll probably be prime minister one day, if not queen. I must make sure I'm living in Australia by then).

Anyway, I decided to leave her to it, and went back outside to have a look around for silly names. It was a bit spooky in the grave-

QVEEN HANNAH☹

yard on my own so I walked up onto the top of the Roman bank right next to the church. On the other side there's a steep drop with a path at the bottom, really creepy and gloomy. When I looked down, I swear it's not a lie, I saw a huge black dog!!!!! It was running along, not looking to left or right, and its breath was all steamy. Honestly it's the truth! I wanted to run away but I was scared that if I moved it would see me. But it just carried on running and disappeared into the shadows. I rushed back down the bank and found the others, my heart thumping, and Mum said, 'Are you all right? You look like you've seen a ghost!' I just said I was cold and could we go home.

I was scared thinking about it in the car until I remembered I'd seen the St Christopher painting. When we got back I looked him up on the computer and its true, he is supposed to protect you from bad things – if you believe in that stuff. But I kind of think that if you're dealing with a scary ghost dog it's probably a good idea to have a magical saint on your side. Why let facts get in your way?

RARGH!

YIKES!

GO, ST CHRIS!

**

Lucky for you, you can't smell me, that's all I can say. Well, actually I can say quite a lot <u>more</u> than that! For example:

MUD SUCKS!
And
IT'S NOT FAIR!!
And
WHY ME?

I have had a shower and everything but I can still smell the mud, it's stuck up my nostrils. It's been a traumatic day. And all we were doing was looking for butterflies. Pretty safe, you might think.

There's this place we went to called Wheat Fen (**BLACK SHUCK MONITOR** : No sightings! **OTHER SPOOKS**: Ghost free!) which is special because you can see these huge butterflies called Swallowtails that don't live in other parts of England.

103

They actually look a bit like small birds, they're so big. This is the only time of year you can see them - so there were quite a few people out on the fen, looking through binoculars and telescopes.

HEE HEE!

BEHIND YOU!

The Swallowtails like it there because they are very fussy about their food and the two things they find tasty happen to grow there. The caterpillars eat one plant, and one plant only, called milk-parsley, and then when they turn into butterflies they only really like nectar from pink/purple flowers.

Obviously Swallowtail mums aren't very strict. I can just imagine what my mum would say if I decided I was only going to eat food of one colour. Imagine...

Me: I'm not going to eat any more peas, broccoli or spinach because they are GREEN and I shall be only eating YELLOW things from now on: bananas, butter and custard, please.

Mum: Eat your greens or there'll be no computer for a week.

Me: Oh. OK. Mmm, this spinach is really yummy..(a lie...).

Anyway, we walked along this path to where the milk-parsley and pink flowers grow, and kept looking and looking over the reed bed. Lots of dragonflies were whizzing about like remote control helicopters up and down the ditch. They kept crashing into each other (someone somewhere needs practise with the remote control).

Then suddenly one of the blokes with binoculars got all excited, and shouted 'One coming through!' and this huge yellow and black butterfly fluttered by in front of us. It was amazingly big - someone said their wing span is 10cm!

After that we saw quite a few but they fly really fast, and all over the place, as if they're a bit drunk on the nectar, so they were quite hard to follow. That was my problem. One came bombing along this narrow little path in between the reeds (which were as high as my head) and I was running after it, shouting at the others to follow me, keeping my eyes on the butter-fly, not really looking where I was going... Then WHAM! next thing I knew I was face down in a ditch of dis-gusting black mud. I don't know how it happened, but it hurt, and it was cold, and the stench from the marsh mud was like:

a)   rotten eggs
b)   a sewage works
c)   the smelliest smelly thing in smelly land

Correct answer: all of them, especially c)

Hannah and Lil laughed and laughed and laughed. They laughed so much that a small crowd gathered to see what was so funny, and they all laughed as well. Everyone's binoculars turned my way and the laughter rang around the whole fen. I felt about as small as a Swallowtail caterpillar (which, by the way, looks like a piece of bird poo).

SPOT THE DIFFERENCE

CATERPILLAR

POO

I wanted to go home immediately - obviously - but my cruel parents just wanted to stay a bit longer, to just see another one or two butterflies, and they said that if my trousers were wet I should take them off. TAKE THEM OFF???!!! IN PUBLIC??? ARE THEY MAD???!!!

In the end I dripped back to the car on my own and sat in the front seat listening to the radio. When the others finally came back, instead of being kind and sympathetic, they all went 'poo you stink!', 'quick open the windows', and 'Oh, Jim, didn't you get to the loo in time?' etc etc.

I did, for once, get to sit in the front on the way home - I'd dripped on the seat and made a nasty brown stain. So Dad decided he would really rather have a nap in the back. Result!

JULY

Blimey! June was almost monster-free and I was thinking maybe I'd got a bit hysterical about the whole Black Shuck thing - it's possible I suppose that the Hell Hound I saw at Caistor was just a big black dog off its leash - and I was hoping that maybe Norfolk isn't as full of spooky beasts as I'd imagined. But today Ranworth proved me wrong. To start with:

BLACK SHUCK MONITOR: A large black dog is supposed to guard some treasure buried by the monks of St. Benet's Abbey nearby, under the gateway to the Old Hall - we kept well clear of there.

OTHER SPOOKS: Another monk from St Benet's can sometimes be heard praying in the church, and people have also heard him rowing across Ranworth Broad. Plus on December 31st the devil is seen riding across the Broad with the soul of a man

under his arm. What does a soul
look like I wonder? You'd
think it would be
all kind of
wispy and
ghosty, so
not that
easy to

hold, especially on a horse galloping over
some water - but I suppose the devil has
had a lot of practise. I wonder if the devil
and the monk ever bumped into each
other?

But also - DRAGONS!!!. Loads of them...

Anyway, my cousins Bill (mad) and Julie
(bossy) are on a cruise boat on the
Norfolk Broads this week so we went to
see them today, at Ranworth. When we
got there Uncle John was all red faced
because he'd driven the boat over a rope
and it had tangled up the rudder - they'd

had to be towed by another boat the last bit of the journey. Auntie Ann was really cross because she'd tried to warn him about the rope but he'd had his I-Pod up too loud and didn't hear her. Bill and Julie were desperate to escape, so us lot went off with ice creams, leaving Mum and Dad cheering up Auntie Ann with cake from the tea shop, while Uncle John tried to untangle the rope with a stick.

My cousins had never been there before so the first place we took them to was the visitor centre. You have to walk along a boarded path that's built over a bog. No, not *that* sort! Although it *is* a bit pongy.

Julie's a little bit younger than Lil, so my sister got the chance to use my teasing techniques on her. One of the information signs says the bog is a 'swamp without alligators'. But Lil told Julie that this was a cover-up and that in fact huge alligator-like creatures had been seen there by lots of people. Julie said that was stupid because you don't get alligators in England.

Without blinking an eye Lil said the alligators had been released there illegally by someone who'd kept them as pets but found them too fierce to look after. I was impressed by her quick thinking - but then she has had the best teacher (i.e. me).

She pointed out the sign which said the swamp was 'treacherously wet and boggy' and said this was to prevent people stepping off the board-walk because one little girl, about the size of Julie, had stepped off and been dragged under by a monstrous waiting alligator, never to be seen again. It had all been hushed up by the government. There's was a nasty smell and Bill said it was because the alligators had eaten a couple of old ladies earlier and got indigestion.

Bill's a bit bigger than me, and he thought it was really funny to keep trying to push me off the path into the mud, while Hannah made stupid alligator-like roaring noises. Luckily the marshy bit only lasts a short while and then you get to the visitor centre which is this little thatched building that floats. You have to go over a kind of draw-bridge to get to it.

Upstairs there are some binoculars and telescopes to look at the birds on the

Broad. Hannah did her whole twitcher thing, and told us the names of everything. There was definitely a heron but the other birds had silly names like Funny Turn and Wobbler. I might have remembered them wrong though.

My cousin Julie went up to the woman running the shop and asked her if it was true about alligators in the marshy bit. I thought, 'aha, this is when Lil gets found out.' But no! The woman said, well she'd never seen one, but she'd noticed bubbles coming up from under the mud sometimes and wondered what that was. And then she said the diving birds go under water for ages and ages, and she's sure that sometimes they never come up again, and maybe the alligators were eating them.

EEK!

THEN she sort of went 'Oh!' as if someone had poked her with a pin, and she
asked us if we'd been to the church yet
and we said no, and she said 'you might
find something there that could prove there
really is some kind of monster here.' I
thought, Oh, great. Another weirdo.
Obviously we asked her what she meant
about the church but she just winked at
us a bit and said we should look at some
of the pictures there.

We went back up to the binoculars bit
and watched the birds diving for quite a
long time to see if any of them disappeared. None of them did which I was glad
about. Then we saw two women with wild
hair, and two old fat
blokes waving at us madly
from a boat, and
realised it was our
parents. They'd had a
trip on the little electric

boat ferry from near the cafe and I was really jealous. But quite glad to see them, because I thought that, given a choice, a monster alligator would probably choose Uncle John for its lunch rather than me. Let's just say there's <u>more</u> of him. Especially after we'd had our picnic and he ate a whole pork pie.

After that we went to the church. You can go up the tower which was cool. It says there are 89 steps but I counted 90 and Lil was sure there were only 87. Anyway, at the top of the steps there are two ladders and then a trapdoor you have to push open. And then you're on the top of the roof and can see for miles - you could see Happisburgh Lighthouse just sticking up in the very far distance. And you could see the Old Hall - but no black dog. And across the water - but no rowing monk. I looked down into the churchyard and felt quite sick - it is a long way

down and it would hurt. A
lot. Luckily Mum didn't
come up, otherwise she'd
have started screaming
at me not to throw
myself off.

We went down
again, and wandered
around inside looking for something that
was about monster alligators. There's a
wooden screen across the middle with
paintings of saints on, which Mum said was
a rude screen. The people painted on it all
had their clothes on and no-one was sticking their tongue out so I didn't get what
she meant. But after laughing at me hysterically for several minutes - which I
thought was mean of her - she said that
'rood' is an old English word for 'cross' -
but not the cross which means 'angry', but
the cross like 'two large wooden sticks
nailed together'. Well, why didn't she say

that in the
first place?
(Actually, I
still didn't
know what the
heck she was
going on about
but I tried to
look interested).

CROSS 1

GRRR!

CROSS 2

What I did notice was how many
pictures of dragon's there were - it's like
the place is obsessed with monsters. There
was a picture of George and the Dragon -
which you often see in churches - but then
there was another dragon with seven heads,
and another with a woman sticking a spear
in one, and then another by the war
memorial. I wondered if that was what the
weirdo woman at the shop had meant us
to see, and maybe she thought the monster
in the swamp was a dragon. But then I
heard Julie let out a scream from near the

door. I thought maybe she'd seen the monk - but she was looking at a kind of box on the wall with a light behind it which lit up some pictures. They were photos from a big book that was made for the church 500 hundred years ago. And this is what one of them showed:

It's the truth! We were all quite scared by then, and I was very glad I wasn't sleeping on a boat on the Broad that night. Bill said it was all a silly story, but I could see he was nervous. We went and had a cup of tea in the little cafe next to the church, and felt a bit better after some cake.

But then we went back to the boat, and Uncle John put Radio Norfolk on. And the first song we heard? 'See you later alligator. In a while crocodile...'

I'm telling you!

***

If your Mum said 'we're going to the Henry blog museum today' you'd think it was something to do with some bloke called Henry writing on the internet about his life or whatever, and you'd wonder why there was a museum about it. Wouldn't you? I don't know why my Mum thinks it's so hilarious when I make these understandable mis-takes. She should make herself clearer.

Anyway, after she'd laughed at me for several minutes, she explained that Blogg is a Norfolk surname, and that Henry Blogg was a famous lifeboat

man - one of the bravest men who ever lived, according to the museum we went to in Cromer.

I like Cromer. There's a good beach and lots of places to buy ice cream. It's about the only place in Norfolk where you get good waves, and there are always surfers waiting on their boards around by the pier, even if you go in winter. It was really hot, so we spent most of our time on the beach, and I managed to catch a few good waves on the body board. Dad surfed with me for quite a long time, got exhausted and feel asleep on the beach

with no suntan lotion on. We had a competition afterwards to describe most accurately what he looked like.

Answers

LOBSTER

Hannah: a boiled lobster (5/10: for lack of originality)

Lil: a strawberry jelly (7/10: good on texture but unrealistically red)

JELLY

Mum: oh, you silly twit, quick put your shirt on! (disqualified)

BEEFBURGER

Me: an uncooked burger (10/10 because that's exactly what his back looked like).

We went to the Blogg museum to get out of the sun for a bit. There's a statue of Henry Blogg up on the cliff which I'd seen before, and just thought it was some old bloke who'd lived there. He doesn't look like a hero. But apparently when he wasn't hiring out deckchairs or fishing for crabs (glamorous!), he was mostly rowing - rowing! - out in dangerous seas and saving hundreds of sailors from drowning. I think he must have changed into the clothes of a super-hero when no-one was looking, but I can't think of a good super-hero name. What about...

[American accent]
Is it a bird??
Is it a plane??? No!
It's SUPER SHRIMP!!!

DON'T YOU FRET!

Which would fit in well with the silly names of the other old lifeboat men - I read some in the museum. Imagine...

You're on a sinking ship, the waves are like mountains, crashing over the side, the wind is howling, the deck heaving as if you're on a big dipper. You manage to crawl to the radio and croak: 'Mayday, mayday, we're sinking fast. Help! Come as quick as you can!' and then - at last! - a thin little voice comes crackling down the line:

'Don't you fret yourself, laddy! Boy Primo, Pimpo and Shrimp are on their way.'

You wouldn't feel very happy, would you? (and I didn't make those names up).

When it cooled off a bit in the evening we got fish and chips and walked along to the end of the pier to see the real lifeboat. Suddenly there was an emergency and all these lifeboat men came running and jumped into the boat. It was dead exciting! Someone shouted, 'All clear' and then the boat went swoosh! down this long slope, and crashed into the waves - it looked like the best water chute ever!

I said how it must be cool being a
lifeboat man, and Hannah went all soppy
and said how romantic it would be, to be
washed out to sea and saved by such
brave men, and then my Mum got really
cross and said how silly Hannah
was and then ranted on and on
about how there would be
nothing romantic about
being freezing cold and
wet and shivering and
half drowned with
crabs pinching your toes

WHERE ARE YOU
SUPER SHRIMP?

and hypothermia, and your fingers falling
of with frostbite...[I felt I had to step in
there and say I didn't think it was quite
that cold, but Mum ignored me]...and the
terrible loneliness in the dark thinking
about how your family and friends would
miss you, and the waves, and the salt
making sores on your skin, and the terrible
thirst...

And then I butted in and said 'and after all that suffering and misery and torture, the lifeboat would turn up and a little old voice would sail over the roaring wind saying:

'Don't you fret there, my gal. Boy Primo, Pimpo and Shrimp are here!''

[Jim's Rule 1 of comedy: If a jokes worth telling, it's worth telling twice.]

Hannah didn't think it was funny but my Dad choked on his chips laughing. Mum slapped him on the back meaning to help, but she'd forgotten his sun burn and he let out a terrible howl of pain, and threw the rest of his chips all over the old lady standing next to him. While Dad was grovelling around on the floor clearing up the mess and Mum was picking chips out of the bewildered old lady's hair, me and the girls crept back onto the pier and pretended we didn't know them.

There's a theatre next to the lifeboat station on the pier. On the way down to see the lifeboat I'd been busy eating my chips and hadn't noticed it, but while we were hanging about waiting for M&D we were stood outside it and I suddenly realised that the place was covered in pictures of huge, snarling black dogs – because they were putting a play on of 'The Hound of the Baskervilles'!!!! Spooky coincidence or what!!??

I picked up a leaflet and began to read it and – maybe it was just because it was getting a bit late by then – I suddenly felt a bit cold. It said that the play was being put on by a local theatre group because

Conan Doyle got the idea for 'The Hound of the Baskervilles' when he was STAYING IN CROMER!! He was told all about Black Shuck whilst visiting his posh friend at the Hall, who said the Hell Hound used to run along the cliff here and through the Hall's garden.

M&D caught up with us at that point and I showed them the leaflet which they thought was interesting - so on our way home we drove past Cromer Hall to see

what it looked like. It was beginning to get dark by then, but from the road we could see this huge flint hall, with turrets and pointy windows like something out of a horror movie. And, just before we drove off, a ghostly white Barn Owl flew across the lawn in front. I was glad we were safely in the car.

When we got home we checked the Cromer lifeboat blog (there must be a joke there somewhere) and it said they'd successfully rescued a kite surfer who'd been washed out to sea. There's a gallery of the lifeboat men on the website and I was disappointed to see they all had very normal names like Paul and Craig. Not even one 'Fishy' amongst them. I also checked to see if there was any more detail about the Black Shuck connection:

BLACK SHUCK MONITOR: Black Shuck runs between Overstrand and Cromer every night, and has been seen several times on the beach and in the lanes nearby!! Once it tried to drown a child who was swimming in the sea - glad I didn't know that this morning. In Overstrand there is even a place called Shuck's Lane!!! That makes it <u>official</u>.

AUGUST

Summer hols! Whoopee!!

We've been away for a couple of weeks in Cornwall. We stayed on a farm and made friends with the family there and they let us help with the animals and stuff it. It was cool. And we did lots of surfing. Dad spent the whole time in a full wet suit, with any visible part covered in full strength white sun tan lotion - so now we've nicknamed him 'The Manatee'. The similarity is remarkable.

Strangely, he doesn't like his new name.

Back now though and my Gran is staying with us. The plan was, she would take us to the beach every day this week but today was too wet and windy. So she decided we were going to do something she'd like, and took me and Lil to a museum and a church.

She said Mum used to love going to museums with her when she was a girl. Poor Mum - she's done well, really, to be as nearly normal as she is.

It's not fair though, because Hannah loves museums but she'd gone to the library with a friend to work on a chemistry project. I tried desperately to organise something else but none of my mates were at home.

Luckily the museum in Swaffham was only small and was mostly about Egyptian mummies and curses and stuff. There were some other strange things in there that had been found in the area. In one display cabinet there were some fossils - shrimp, fish, scallop sea urchin, devil's toe nail. Hang on a minute. DEVIL'S TOE NAIL??

No explanation. As if it's perfectly
normal to display bits that have
dropped off supernatural beings.

   We went passed a big
stained glass window in there
of the pedlar of Swaffham 'who did by a
dream find great treasure.' Apparently this
poor man, who sold stuff on the street in
Swaffham, had a dream that he should go
to London Bridge to find gold, so he went
there, didn't find any, got chatting to a
shop keeper, in the pub probably, who said,
'I had this funny dream, about a bush in
the back garden of a poor man in
Swaffham, and underneath the bush there
was a pot of gold.' The pedlar probably
choked on his crisps, before saying 'Oh
really? Dreams are so silly though, aren't
they', with his fingers crossed. And then he
ran all the way back to Swaffham. Dug
up the bush. Found a pot of gold. Two
actually.

I can't help feeling it would have been simpler if he'd just dreamed where the pot of gold was in the first place instead of having to go all the way to London, find the right bloke, and then come all the way back again.

Anyway, it is a true story because the pedlar was suddenly rich, and he paid for building part of the church - we went and had a look later, and there's a carving of him on one of the bench ends. I wish I had dreams like that.

SNORE!
YUM!
SNORE!

The museum has got lots of stuff about Egypt and mummies etc because the man who found the tomb of Tutankhamun came from Swaffham. We watched a short film, like something out of Indiana Jones, which was quite cool. And there were instructions on how to write your name using *hyro*... i mean *hiro*... No, I mean *hieroglyphics*. That's it! These took us about five minutes:

It must have been hard to write a note in a hurry in those days. ~~Especially if~~ your name was Tutankhamun. I expect he got called 'Toot' for short.

Lil showed a worrying interest in how to make a mummy - there were instructions on how to take out internal organs, embalm a corpse and so on. I thought it might be a good idea to interrupt her. There was a model of a mummy up one corner, and I went, 'Oh my God, it moved!'

She was out of there, and standing in the street in less than five seconds. Genius.

TIDY YOUR ROOM!

We were supposed to be having a picnic but Gran had forgotten to bring it. So instead she gave us each a couple of quid and told us to go round a small supermarket in Swaffham and be grown-up and buy ourselves a sensible lunch. Guess who bought what:

Picnic 1: packet of bacon flavoured crisps, bag of marshmallows, chewing gum, can of coke
Picnic 2: packet of jelly babies, packet of jammy dodgers, bottle of fizzy orange
Picnic 3: wholemeal roll, cheese, apple, bottle of water.

Answers: Picnic 1, me: Picnic 2, Gran ; Picnic 3, Lill

Gran said Lil wasn't normal and children should eat a lot of sweets to grow up healthy and strong. Have I mentioned that my Gran is a bit weird?

MORE JELLY BABIES!

Afterwards we drove off into the countryside to find this church Gran had read about. She'd marked it on the map but we got lost anyway, and seemed to be going down one tiny lane after another, in circles, never seeing any houses or people or other cars. Which is just as well because Gran drives like a maniac - I think she'd had too much fizzy drink, and she was feeding herself jelly babies with one hand and holding the map in the other. I was beginning to think we might be lost forever, but suddenly she went 'Aha!' and swerved up a track.

I think the Saxons were probably being sarcastic when they called the place Houghton-on-the-Hill. Houghton-on-the-pimple might have been more accurate.

pimple

Anyway, it's a spooky kind of place, a small church surrounded by trees, and a bumpy field where the old village once stood. Gran said the village disappeared after most of the people got killed by the Black Death. The reason for us coming was to see some paintings on the walls which are like a thousand years old - they're the oldest wall paintings in Europe, she said (she reminds me a lot of Hannah, or is it the other way round? They both like telling you stuff).

BLACK SHUCK MONITOR: Houghton-on-the-pimple is next to the Peddars Way which Black Shuck travels along at night searching for his master. Luckily, Gran didn't make us go there at night time.
OTHER SPOOKS: No need to look this up on the web - Lil saw it!!

It turns out the church is haunted - there's a photo in the church of a lady standing in the doorway and behind her is a shadowy figure - it's very clear. It's supposed to be a monk that used to live here.

BEHIND YOU!

Loads of people have seen it. Gran said that was all a lot of nonsense, but the man who was looking after the church said he'd seen the monk several times and lots of other people have too.

After that I felt a bit funny, but that might partly have been because Lil attached herself to my arm and wouldn't let go. She said she was protecting me from the ghost but I'm not so sure. Then the man told us how a few years ago the church had been a ruin and strange people used to come here to worship the devil and spooky stuff. There's a big cross outside which is supposed to scare them off. That made Lil cling even tighter. And then we looked at the paintings. They didn't help.

It took a while to understand what all the
pictures were - there was quite a cool one
of an angel with a turban playing a trum-
pet. Random. And
a row of
saints looking
grumpy -
being holy
doesn't look
much fun.

They look like they're holding tea-towels
- Gran said they didn't have dishwashers in
those days, so maybe they were fed-up
about having to do all the drying up?

On the right hand side Gran pointed out
this really weird
demon. It was bald
with great big ears
and staring white
eyes, and was stick-
ing its tongue out at

Jesus, a bit like a mad Mickey Mouse. And there was another one next to him which wasn't so clear but you could see its sharp teeth. A scary dog?? Had they seen something like it running along the Peddar's Way at night? Perhaps that's why the village got deserted. Not Black Death, but Black Shuck??

HEE HEE!

There was also a bit that showed people falling into hell, and on the left hand side which was supposed to be more cheerful, there were pictures of dead people rising out of their coffins. They weren't smiling either. I think everyone was pretty depressed in those days - people probably didn't know what a smile looked like, living as they did in dark hovels, with the Black Death and no telly.

By this time I'd lost all feeling in my arm because my sister was clinging on so tight she'd stopped the blood in it. She kept saying 'I don't like it' and Gran kept saying, 'oh, don't be so silly. Why don't you go outside and play?'

So we went outside but although there are lots of flowers and stuff, it **is** a graveyard, and it **is** where the ghost was photographed. You know that feeling you get when you think something's creeping up behind you, and your neck feels all funny? The hairs on my neck were trembling. Lil was like a wobbling jelly by this time, and kept whimpering. I think I prefer her when she's angry and armed with a stick.

While we were driving home which took hours - Gran's idea of a short cut seemed to involve driving twice as far as necessary but at 100 miles an hour - Lil confessed that she was sure she'd seen the ghost, flitting around the corner of the church as we came out of the door. I think she'd eaten too much cheese. That would explain the funny smells in the car as well. Or that might have been something to do with Gran and the whole packet of jammy dodgers she'd eaten mixed up with the fizzy orange. I'm not sure. Another unsolved mystery.

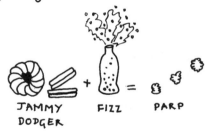

JAMMY DODGER   FIZZ   PARP

***

It was hot today so Gran took us to Waxham beach. It hasn't got shops or a pier, but it has got a nice sandy beach and dunes that you can run about in. It's only a little way up the coast from Horsey and when we were swimming a seal came

along to see what we
were up to. It was a
bit scary when it dis-
appeared underwater
and I thought it might
fancy a nibble of my
toes. Gran thought it was
hilarious to keep singing the
Jaws theme at us:
Nuuuuur-nuh! Nuuuuur-nuh!
Nur-nuh-Nur-nuh-Nur-nuh-Nur-nuh!
NurnuhNurnuhNurnahNurnah!!!

But Lil said she wasn't scared because
the seal was one of the babies we'd seen
in January, and that she and it were
friends. The seal was called 'Fluffy'
apparently. I said I thought the seal would
probably have a name more like 'Errgh' or
'Orrgh', which are the only sounds I've ever
heard them making, but she said that
'Fluffy' and the other seals speak at a
very high frequency that only children

under eight can hear, because as you get older your ears get tired and can't hear so well.

Hannah said it was frightening what rubbish a little science and a seven year old brain can produce and I had to agree with her, for once. Gran said there was nothing wrong with her ears,

ERRGH!

HE SAYS HELLO, HOW ARE YOU, AND HAVE YOU GOT ANY FISH?

thank you very much, though sometimes she could hardly believe what she was hearing. And then she muttered something about Lil and her 'fantasy world' and 'needs therapy' which I though was a bit hard on Lil considering Gran had spent half the morning going 'Nur-nuh Nur-nuh!' really loudly and people had been giving her funny looks.

Gran had forgotten the picnic again so for lunch we had to walk round to the big

barn where there's a cafe. It's a very big
barn, one of the biggest in the country.
You can go inside it, which was nice and
cool, and there are loads of birds flitting
in and out from under the
roof - Hannah
(prize
TWIT-
cher) said
they were
swifts and
Gran said
'yes, they <u>are</u>
very fast' and
Hannah said in a loud voice
'NO, THEY'RE CALLED SWIFTS
GRAN!!' and Gran said, 'I know. They <u>are</u>
very fast. No need to shout, dear. Nothing
wrong with my ears, thank you very much.'

We had some really nice cake sitting
outside watching the swifts and laying bets
on whether the people sitting at the table

nearest the barn would get pooed on.
Nobody did though. Hannah went inside the
barn to pretend she didn't know us, and
came back saying there was some interesting stuff in there about bats and owls,
and a mad owner from the past called
'Old Barney'. I had a look and there's a
story that he once tricked the Devil; that
he wrestled with chimney sweeps; held New
Years Eve dinners for the ghosts of his
dead ancestors; and murdered his wife.
Random!

What was more worrying: Gran read a
bit of the guide book which said that Old
Barney's son had a pack of hounds that
made such a racket they could be heard
for miles around - and they were kept so
hungry that once they killed and ate their
keeper...Urgh! (not the name of a seal, by
the way).

It got me thinking though - maybe that's where the story of scary mad ghost dogs might have come from? And maybe one or two of them escaped, and its their great, great, great, great, great, great, great, great, great, great, great, great, grand-pups that people sometimes see? Less scary than a ghost dog anyway.

BLACK SHUCK MONITOR: no sightings - but see above.

OTHER SPOOKS: devils, ghosts, murderers, the whole lot.

SEPTEMBER

Back to school this week. Boo!!! As usual the weather turned really hot and sunny as soon as I got my school sweatshirt out of the cupboard. So at the weekend we pretended we were still on holiday and went to Castle Acre with a picnic - luckily Mum is better at remembering than Gran.

BLACK SHUCK MONITOR: The village is on the Peddar's Way, which the dog runs up and down. I felt a bit funny when I read that there'd been a sighting in the village as recently as 1983
OTHER SPOOKS: no sightings!

On a sunny day it didn't seem too scary. We sat by the river to eat the picnic. The river is very clear and we could see some quite big fish that were floating very still in the current, just waggling their tails now and again. Dad said he'd caught fish like that using his bare hands when he was 'a lad'. The idea was to get your hand under and flip them up in the air. So we all lay on the bank and slid our hands in, really quietly,

HEE HEE HEE!

but the fish just moved to the side slightly, or darted off. Lil said that she could hear them laughing with her supersonic young ears (maybe Gran was right about the therapy..?).

We all said that Dad had made it up about catching the fish and he got cross and told us a long story about how he'd caught one when he was a boy scout and cooked it over a fire and how it had been the best meal he'd ever eaten - but then Mum said she'd never heard him tell that story before, and he got really grumpy, and said that was because 'she never lis- tened when he was telling her his boy scout stories'. And then things got serious - he started rolling his trousers up.

Mum said it was too deep to paddle but he said it wasn't and sat on the bank and slid in, and then let out a kind of whooaAAHH!!! noise as the cold water went right up over his knees and made his trousers all wet! HA HA! and then he couldn't get out again. HA HA HA!!!

whooAHHH!

He got really muddy, trying to scramble up the bank and let out quite a few rude words, which I have replaced with the word 'BANANA' in the following extract:

'Oh BANANA! its freezing, aahh, oh, BANANA, my trousers, its gone all up my BANANA legs, aah, why don't you BANANA help me, you BANANAS!'

We all had hysterics. Funnily enough the fish had all disappeared by the time we finally pulled him out. Luckily (or unluckily for us as we had to look at his knobbly knees) he'd brought some spare shorts.

SCARY KNEES →

So then we walked up to the ruined castle. We had a really good game of Normans and peasants which involved me and Lil (Norman lords) charging down the banks and attempting to knock over M&D & Hannah (miserable peasants). Hannah was really annoying and kept saying how 'historically inaccurate' we were being, so she got knocked down the most:

Hannah: They wouldn't have run down the...Aahh! (she is taken down by Lil's expert rugby tackle)
Lil: Mon dieu! You are one smelly peasant!

Hannah: But Mum, tell them! The peasants wouldn't have...OOph! (she is taken down by my excellent 'steam train' technique)

Me: You meeserable leetle peasant worm. Surrender!

Hannah: And they wouldn't have spoken like...OOwww! (she is taken down by my highly skilled tripping technique No.1)

TRIP TECHNIQUE 1.

Me: Let's take the meeserable peasant to the dungeon until she promise to be less - 'ow you say? - boring!!

Hannah: I'm not being boring, I'm just pointing out that...AArrgh! (My less successful tripping technique no. 2 fails and we are danger - ously open to attack). Right, you've had it you horrible pair!

Lil: AAAHHH! Mummy! Help!! I don't like

it!!AAHHHH! (Lil is taken down by Hannah and suffers the 'two hands under the armpits' tickling torture for several minutes while I make a brave retreat up the hill)

Mum to Dad: Isn't it sweet seeing them playing together so nicely?

After Lil had surrendered we all walked into the village for a cup of tea and cake, which I expect the French invaders probably also did - although p'raps they would have had gateaux - as it's thirsty work invading.

AH! A LOVELY CUP OF YOUR INGLEESH TEA!

***

It seems to me that Norfolk is infested with supernatural beings, and it's surprising that we don't all stay locked up safely in our houses (with an x-box preferably) instead of going out all the time to visit places where we might be savaged by a large ghost dog, or eaten by a man-eating alligator or burnt to ash by a dragon. I wonder sometimes whether M&D are secretly trying to get rid of us.

NORFOLK

So today they took us to a place called Ludham where there is an almost definitely true story about a dragon living there - although in the story they call it the 'Ludham worm' - which makes you wonder how big the birds were in the old days...

BLACK SHUCK MONITOR / OTHER SPOOKS Who cares? There's a real dragon!!!

We stopped for a cup of coffee in the cafe opposite the church and I noticed a great big stone just outside it, and I asked the waitress what it was and - as matter-of-fact as if she was telling me it rained on Tuesday - she said, 'oh, that's the stone they used to block up the Dragon's tunnel.' She did!

She said, it was reported in a newspaper 200 years ago that this worm was 5 feet 8 inches long (173cm), and was almost 3 feet (100cm) around its stomach and it had a long snout and horns on its head: or, in other words, it was a DRAGON!!!!!!

DRAGON ATE MY HAMSTER!

TRUTHFINDER

Reporter and top scientist **Jim Truthfinder** seeks out the truth behind the mysterious legend of the Ludham Dragon.

Worm

People have trembled in their beds for centuries, in fear that the dreaded Ludham worm might return to terrorise their village.

Jeering

Local know-it-all Hannah Smarty-pants suggested that the so-called monster was in fact probably an escaped Boa-constrictor but, as the jeering crowd pointed out to her, this was highly unlikely 200 years ago in Norfolk.

Scary

Small, scared girl, Lil I-dont-like-it, stated her opinion, very quietly, that it must have been a scary monster from the underworld, but she was quickly contradicted by Professor Mum who pointed out that it was a silly story made to sell the newspaper.

Filthy

However, Jim Truthfinder, winner of the 'Honest Bloke Award', and top scientist, strongly disagreed with this filthy slur on newspaper reporters, and said that if it had been published in the newspapers it must be true.

Stunning

But the arguments were silenced by the stunning revelation made by Mr Dad:

Ranworth church, scene of the giant man-eating alligator picture, is just across the river from Ludham!

Monsters

This extensive scientific research proves beyond doubt that there have been scary monsters in these parts for centuries!

Next week's exclusive: Jim Truthfinder seeks out the facts about the Tooth fairy...

157

We only went to Ludham on our way to somewhere with a lot of windmills known as How Hill. Its full name should be: How-could-anyone-call-this-a-Hill. It makes you wonder whether people saw things different-

PIMPLE

ly in the old days - what with six foot long worms, and hills that are about as high as the average baby's elbow.

Apparently, they drank beer for breakfast. That might explain it.

There's a cottage you can visit at How-could-anyone-call-this-a-Hill called Toad Hole Cottage. I thought that 'toad hole' was a bit harsh. It looked quite cosy, all set out like it would have been in Victorian times. But upstairs there were only two bedrooms, and the kids used to have to sleep in the same bed, head to toe. Lil said she would rather sleep under the bed than be squashed in the middle between me and Hannah and our cheesy toes, and Hannah said she would rather sleep outside under a bush than sleep with my smelly feet next to her nose and I said I would rather sleep standing up in the broom cupboard with the spiders than risk suffocation from the stench of her pongy feet...and then we had to ask ourselves the question: do spiders have pongy feet? Because if they do that would be a lot of smelly feet x 8 wriggling around in the cupboard with me. So I said, ok I would rather sleep in the bath - but Mum pointed out to me that there wasn't a proper bath, just a kind of large tin bucket you had to sit in. So then I got a bit stuck for ideas, and we went and looked at the windmills.

There are three, although only one looks like a proper brick windmill - the others are made out of wood. Mum did the whole lecture about wind pumps again.

She had failed to remember **Jim's Rule 1 of comedy:** If a joke's worth telling, it's worth telling twice. This was too great an opportunity to miss. So I went into this brilliant comedy routine about windpumps:

'One wind pump would surely be bad enough, ladies and gentlemen, but three could be dangerous! Especially if you're sleeping head to toe! '
(Pause for laughter)
'....I mean, I've heard marshes get gassy but three pumps is beyond a joke! '
(another pause for laughter and applause)...

PARDON!

'Dear oh dear! And Mum - You really like windpumps, don't you? So now I understand why you like Dad! Ooph! ...'
(Pause for me to recover my breath after being thrown to the floor by a violent member of the audience i.e. Dad)...

By the way, <u>Jim's Rule 2 of comedy</u> is: there is only one rule. ~~Except~~ for <u>Jim's Rule 3 of comedy</u> which is: don't make rude jokes about people if they are standing near enough to take you down.

EXCUSE ME!

Now. On the way back, we stopped off at another church. We all went 'no, please, no, not another, it's too much, please no, anything but

OOPS!

another church - a windpump even - anything! Please no...' etc but M&D didn't seem to be able to hear us. So we trooped in after them and then things went really weird.

Because in that church - which is at HORN-ing - there's a whole collection of carved dragons!!! One shows a man - who looks like an American-Indian - holding a

dragon down under his arm, and another
shows a man being attacked by two
~~HUGE~~ serpents with teeth, and another
shows a dragon with its wings caught in
some wooden stocks, and another - the
scariest - shows a devilish horned creature
feeding someone into the mouth of another
~~HUGE~~ dragon!!! Even Hannah had to
admit that all this monster
stuff was starting to get
serious. There MUST have
been something roaming
around this area in the old
days when it was all marshy
and foggy and damp.

Then Lil found an ancient wooden chest
under a table, all bound in iron, which Mum
said had been made out of one huge tree
trunk. It looked like something out of *Lord
of the Rings*, and I said I thought that the
chest had been made to trap the dragon,
and that it was still in there, waiting for

its moment to escape - when the iron bands finally rusted to pieces, or the wood - which looked rotten - finally crumbled into dust. I put my ear to the lock and I swear I heard it breathing, a kind of rasping 'heeeargh, huuuuuuh, heeeearch, huuuuuuh'.

Or maybe that was just Lil hyperventilating, as she was totally freaked out.

M&D told me to stop winding up my sister or they'd feed me to the dragon. And then we went home.

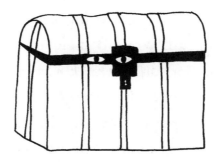

OCTOBER

Oh! My! God! I have just had one of the most disgusting afternoons ever. Mum took Lil, me and my mate Tom to something called a 'funghi foray'. I know what she means now, but before we went she kept saying, 'we're going to a fun guy for a...' and I kept thinking 'What guy?' and 'Why doesn't she ever finish the sentence??' but then I just thought 'Whatever."

I should've taken more notice and then maybe I would've been more ready.

Anyway, what it actually was, was a walk, in a group, around a wood near Holt, looking for different kinds of mushrooms and funguses (or funghi if your posh), led by an expert who could tell us the names of all of them.

The thing is: they are disgusting. Calling them fun-ghi is against the Trades Descriptions Act. They should definitely be called disgustin-ghi. Or possibly pon-ghi

So, anyway, we went off into this first bit of wood which was a kind of clearing and we had to look for any mushroomy things we could find and pick them, so that the expert could identify them - 'cos afterwards he puts all the info on some kind of database for nutters who are obsessed with fungus. Knowing what I know now, I imagine they are all probably vampires or werewolves or evil wizards in their spare time but that's probably unfair. I've had a traumatic afternoon.

Almost the first fungus he showed us was a stinkhorn which looks very rude so I can't draw it, and it was really embarrassing. And it's called the stinkhorn because it gives off the smell of rotting

flesh to attract
flies. It really,
REALLY ponged,
and was
covered in
disgusting slime.
That was just
the beginning.

Me and Tom went
off and looked for stuff and I
found this really good one that was tall
and thin with a black cap that no-one
else had found. I was feeling pleased with
myself until I showed it to the expert and
he said:

'Ahh! Now. That's a good one. But you
might regret picking it without gloves on.
Just smell your fingers.'

And I sniffed them, and got a blast of
full-blown aroma of dog poo. Urrgh! It
turned out the fungus was called Dog

Stinkhorn and it was really, REALLY horrible. I spent the rest of the walk dreaming
about washing my hands - which doesn't
happen often.

We carried on looking - a bit less
enthusiastically - and found all kinds of
weird stuff with silly names like Parrot
Waxcap, Jelly Babies, King Alfred's Cakes,
Yellow Legs....etc. And while we were walking round we invented a pongometer with
measurements of smelliness ranging from
'fresh as a daisy' through to 'death by
stink'. I'm going to stick it on the next
page and put Lil's suggestions in brackets
because they were stupid but she threat-
ened me with a Death Angel fungus if I
didn't write them down.

We argued quite a lot about what the
worst smells in the world were. Mum said it
was my socks which is not fair - they're no
worse than Dad's - so I didn't allow that

SMELL TYPE	E.G.	DOG INDICATOR
FRESH AS A DAISY	A DAISY obviously	1.
NO SMELL	(THE SKY) !?!?	
WHIFFY	CHEESE = Cheddar (Jim's bedroom) *!??!!?*	
SMELLY	ARMPIT OF DAD CHEESE = Stilton	
PONGY	BOILED BROCCOLI It's so wrong! SOUR MILK	
STINKY	CAT/DOG BREATH GOATS CHEESE shouldn't be allowed	
NOXIOUS	SCHOOL TOILETS & OTHER SMELLS AFTER EATING BEANS rhymes with 'part'	
DEATH BY FOUL STENCH	DRAINS/SEWERS (Jim's trainers) fair enough....	

in the Pongometer. Tom reminded me of the time he found his lunchbox after it'd been left in his school bag all summer with a cheese sandwich in it. How could I forget? He held the lunch box under my nose and told me to inhale. I nearly passed out.

Then another disgusting thing happened. We went along the track a bit and were scrambling around looking for stuff and there was this really foul smell and we were thinking 'Blimey, there must be a whole load of Stinkhorn's around here, it really smells like dog poo.' And then we realised that we'd been so busy discussing the pongometer we'd all walked through a HUGE steaming pile of the genuine article, about the size a Hound from Hell would leave after it had eaten that ancient cheese sandwich in Tom's lunch box, and then been very scared. It's put me off my tea just thinking about it. We couldn't get away from the smell after that.

Things only got worse. Possibly the most disgusting bit was when the expert person found what he called the 'egg' of a stinkhorn. Before they grow into the rude shape they start off half underground and look like an egg which he picked up and cut in half so we could see inside. And, while he was explaining it to us, this disgusting slimy jelly was dripping through his fingers and making a horrible squelchy noise. And then he said it was edible!!

No thanks. I will never eat a mushroom again. You don't know where they've been.

BLACK SHUCK MONITOR: I don't want to think about dogs, thanks.

OTHER SPOOKS: None. I expect even they can't stand the stench of the funghi...

***

Wow! I feel like we've just been in a wildlife safari programme like those ones where people get charged by elephants and the camera goes all wobbly and they have to put in a beeeep noise to screen the swear words on the sound track.

We went to this place called Holkham Hall which is up on the coast. But we didn't go on the beach today – too windy. We went for a walk in the park instead, looking for chestnuts.

I've just realised that when people say something they've done was 'a walk in the park', to mean it was really easy, it's very inaccurate. For one thing this walk in the park was quite tiring, and for another thing we got a bit lost, and for

MAKE MY DAY!

another thing, chestnuts are really, REALLY spiky, and for another thing, there were these scary deer lurking round every corner.

COME HERE AND SAY THAT!

As we were walking through the gates into the park we heard this terrible groaning noise, a bit like a lion with stomach ache. I clutched Lil's arm to check she wasn't frightened, and Lil clutched Mum and Mum clutched Dad and Dad clutched Hannah, and then looked a bit embarrassed. Hannah put her 'I'm so clever and you're all miserable dunces' face on and told us it wasn't an escaped lion OR - and she looked at me with a sneer - Black Shuck, OR a dragon or any other kind of mythical beast, but was a deer 'rutting'.

Which makes me think that when people say they're 'in a rut' it's actually something a lot worse than being stuck in a 'groove or furrow caused by wheels' or 'a narrow or predictable way of life' or ' dreary routine' (that's what it says in the dictionary). Oh no. It's much more scary than that.

So anyway, we carried on walking through the trees towards this great big monument that's in the woods there. It's really REALLY tall and has got statues of a sheep and a cow and loads of famous people all round the bottom. Anyway, we were making our way towards it but there was a herd of those deer on the edge of the wood and now and again the terrible groaning noise would come from that direction.

Lil insisted on creeping as near as she could to them and was doing all the usual 'Aahh! Sweeet!' stuff. And then suddenly there was a huge clattering noise as two of the male deer started fighting each other, their antlers all tangled together. They were pushing each other backwards and forwards and banging their head until I got a headache just watching.

They were so wrapped up in fighting they didn't notice us at all, so we crept a bit closer, and then a bit closer, and then a little bit closer. And closer still. And then a tiny bit closer. It went on for ages until the weakest one suddenly lost its balance and got pushed back and back and then it ran away - straight towards us! ARGGH!!

We scattered in all directions. I fell over a bramble and put one hand in a clump of nettles and the other on a pile of well-spiky chestnuts. ARRRGGHHHH!!!

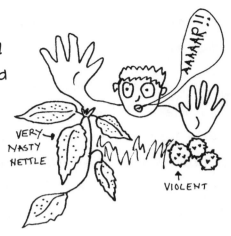

VERY→ NASTY NETTLE

AAAAR!!

VIOLENT

Lil tripped over and ripped her jacket. AAIIEE!!

Dad ran slap-bang into a tree and broke his glasses! BANANA!!!!!!

Mum and Hannah had stayed a sensible distance away on the track - Hannah was watching with binoculars and Mum was videoing it on her phone. Neither of them seemed even a bit worried about us and in fact by the time we'd got up and dusted ourselves down they were having hysterics watching the replay of us screaming and falling over.

Dad can barely see without his glasses so the walk got a bit difficult after that. We walked round the lake and were all glad to see that there were no deer in the area (well, all of us were glad except Dad, who wouldn't have been able to see a deer at that point even if it had come up to him and licked him on the nose). My hands were throbbing and Lil was whining because her jacket had a hole in it. Luckily the cafe was open. It's amazing how eating a piece of cake can stop nettle stings hurting.

YUM!

And that got me thinking again: when people say something is 'a piece of cake', meaning it's easy, it is also very inaccurate. It takes a lot of skill to make a piece of cake. That's why Mum ended up with chocolate spread sandwiches on her birthday instead of the big sponge cake we'd planned. Luckily she never did notice the disappearance of the old cake tin. Or that burn mark on the floor. Or the strange explosion marks inside the oven.

HAPPY BIRTHDAY!

CHOCO SPREAD

BLACK SHUCK MONITOR/ OTHER R SPOOKS: None. A stately home without a ghost? Must be a cover up!

NOVEMBER

So now Hannah's obsession has gone too far. M&D should get her under control. I mean, OK, it's nice that there are lots of birds, and they're not all dead and extinct - but getting up to see them before DAWN!!!! It's not reasonable.

Anyway, that's what we did today. We got to this place called Snettisham at half past six or something in the morning when it was still dark, and then we had to walk quite a long way - maybe twenty minutes - also in the dark. And we hadn't had any breakfast at that point. This was hard enough, but Hannah insisted on lecturing us on what we were going to see.

To be honest I was a bit nervous about being out on the coast while it was dark. Last month was pretty much monster free and I'd started to relax again - but the place we went to this morning was near

King's Lynn and that was where one of the drowned masters of Black Shuck was buried. The dog is supposed to run up and down from there to Great Yarmouth. I didn't mention it to Lil 'cos I thought she'd be scared. I swear as the sun was coming up and I could see better we walked past these enormous paw prints in the mud - they were there for a few metres and then stopped as if the animal had disappeared into thin air!

BLACK SHUCK MONITOR: recent sighting of unexplained large paw prints. I put my shoe next to one and this is what it looked like:

OTHER SPOOKS: Who cares? Just keep the Black Dog with the big paws away from me!!!!

We finally got to this track that ran along a kind of muddy beach, and it got a little bit lighter so you could properly see your hand in front of your face - which was useful because Mum had brought bacon sandwiches. Yum! Things got better after that.

I thought we'd be the only people mad enough to get up so early and walk so far in the middle of nowhere on a freezing cold morning. But NO! There were tons of people there. Most of them had cameras with huge telescopic lenses on them, and they were all set up in a line looking at a great big bank of mud out to sea. After a bit we could see that the tide was coming in, quite fast, covering the mud. Then

there was a sound like a jet engine starting up but it was this HUGE flock of
birds suddenly whooshing up into the sky in
a big black cloud, swirling about like a
swarm of mosquitoes. Hannah told us that
the sea had come in and covered the mud
bank and, because the birds don't like getting their feet wet, they have to fly off.
Hannah was, as usual, being annoyingly
smug about all these facts she knows so I
decided to wind her up a bit.

Me: What are those birds called again?
Hannah: They're nots
Me: What, they haven't got a name?
Hannah: No, they're nots!!
Me: I don't understand. They're not
what?
Hannah: No, you idiot, they ARE nots!!!
Me: But...
Dad: Shut up you two, they're KNOTS
K-N-O-T.

What a stupid name for a bird.

Apparently there might have been 80,000 of them today. That's a lot of knots.

Anyway, these flocks of knots kept swirling around in the sky and then zooming right over our heads to reach a big lake behind us, to wait for the tide to go out again. And, guess what? It was my turn to get pooed on this time - disgusting green poo. Mum said it's good luck to get pooed on by a bird, but does she think I'm stupid or something? I would have been happy for Hannah to have all the 'luck'. And Dad made a very unfunny joke about how he'd often thought I should 'get knot- ted' (it's an ancient form of insult - medieval I think - from when he was young). Oh ha, ha, HA!!

HA!

HA!

HA!

When all the birds had flown over, spreading 'luck' over the whole place, we walked round to a 'hide' (i.e. drafty shed) to look at the knots in the lake. It was quite funny actually. I don't think knots are very clever. They were squeezed onto this sandy bank, making a terrible racket, like a crowd of worried fans all trying to get a view of their favourite celebrity. They were running backwards and for-wards, pushing and shoving, and they sounded really squawky:

Knot 1: Ooh, get your beak out of my ear!
Knot 2: I will if you get your nasty wet rubbery foot off my tail!
Knot 3: Has Gorgeous Gary arrived yet? Where is he?!!
Knot 1: Someone said he's over there!
Knot 2: Quick, everyone, over there. Gorgeous Gary!!!! We love you!
Knot 3: Get out of my way, you big grey lump!

Knot 1: Oi, get your big grey bum out of my face!

Knot 2: No, you get your nasty pointy beak under control!

Knot 3: Where is Gorgeous Gary??!! I must catch a glimpse of him!

Knot 1: Over there! Gorgeous Gary!!!! This way! This way! Over here!

Knot 2: No, no, that way, that way!!

Knot 3: Round in circles!! Quick!!!

ALL KNOTS CHANT: : Gorg-eous Gary!!! Gorg-eous Gary!!!

Knot 1: Aargh!! Watch out for the oyster-catcher!!

Oyster catcher: OI! 'AVE YOU LOT GOT TICKETS??!!!

Oi!-ster catchers are the scary bouncers in the knot world.

   After quite a long wait - during which time I beat Lil several times at noughts and crosses; Hannah embarrassed us by talking to other twitchers and telling them stuff they already knew; and I ate several more bacon sandwiches - these silly birds suddenly all flew off again in great big lines across the sky, back to the sea.

There were so many black dots all moving together, it looked like computer animation - just for a split second, I swear, it looked like a great big black dog. But the others didn't seem to notice, so I didn't say anything.

Just as we were leaving (it felt like a whole day, but was still only 10:30 in the morning) a peregrine falcon (according to Hannah) flew in and the whole flock of knots flew up in one mass, and twisted and turned to get away from the falcon. Pretty cool. The walk back seemed longer in the daylight. The big paw prints had gone.

DECEMBER

Nearly
Christmas!!
Whooppee!!!

   It's been really cold and
snowy so we've been sledging a couple of
times and had some excellent snow ball
fights on the way to school. But now we're
on holiday and Gran has come to stay and
we're doing Christmassy things like decorat-
ing the tree and making mince pies, and
trying to sneak into M&Ds room to see
what they've bought us.

   This afternoon we went to a place
called Felbrigg Hall. The courtyard outside
was all decorated with trees and lights
and stuff, and there were mince pies and
cakes. Which was Christmassy. But it was
really REALLY cold, and then we had to
sing some carols.

The trouble is Gran has got a terrible voice. She thinks she's some kind of prize-winning opera singer with this really REALLY high voice that could be used as a secret weapon (now I know where Lil gets it from). That's bad enough but also she only knows old fashioned versions of the carols. So, for example, we all sang the modern tune for 'I saw three ships' while Gran sang the old tune on her own, over the top, really, REALLY high, with a puzzled look on her face, as if we'd all gone mad. And then she insisted on doing that really high harmony on 'Oh Come All Ye Faithful' which usually happens in the last verse, but she did it in all the verses, and it sounded like someone was standing on a cat's tail.

The other people singing kept looking around, with concerned looks on their faces, to see if the poor animal needed rescuing.

And then we sang 'We Three Kings of Orient Are' and every time we went into the chorus Gran held the note too long:

Us: oh-oh, Star of wonder, star of light
Gran: oooooooh - oooooooooooooooooooh!!!!!

And then sang the whole thing a note behind everyone else as if there was a really bad echo.

I caught Lil's eye, and she giggled, and then I did and then we both had to pretend we were coughing because we couldn't stop giggling, and Mum looked a bit worried and offered us both cough sweets and then we choked on them and were coughing and laughing and crying and had to go and hide in the loos until we'd calmed down.

When we got back, Gran said 'Oh what a shame. You missed a lovely version of Ding Dong Merrily On High' and then 'sang' (more like 'yeowled') at us the bit that goes:

And Dad muttered something like 'it certainly does sound like a bit of a Ding-Dong', and then me and Lil had to run back to the loos again.

But it was after that that the really exciting thing happened. Even though it was dark, Gran insisted that Christmas wouldn't be Christmas if we didn't have a sprig of holly to put on top of the pudding on Christmas day, and she said we couldn't go home until we'd found some holly with berries. M&D said they knew where there was a bit of heath on the way home where they'd seen holly berries before, and we'd go back that way. So off we went in the dark.

There was actually a very bright moon so it wasn't that difficult to see. Hannah, Lil and Gran stayed in the car because it was too cold for them - Gran rolled down the window and kept shouting out helpful hints at us like 'mind out, the leaves might be sharp' and 'haven't you found any yet?', and 'hurry up!' and 'you should eat more carrots!' ??!!

Mum could see some berries quite high up, so she climbed into the branch of a tree nearby, and then tried to clamber onto Dad's shoulders. They had several attempts (I think Mum might have drunk quite a lot of the mulled wine at Felbrigg...) and there was a lot of shrieking and embarrassing behaviour so I wandered off into the little copse of trees.

And there, sitting in a little clearing, with the moon shining straight onto its shiny black fur was - a ~~HUGE BLACK PANTHER~~!!!!!!!

That's what I said:
a ~~HUGE BLACK PANTHER~~!!!!!!!!!!!!!!

I'll say it again:
a HUGE BLACK PANTHER!!!!!!!!!!!!!!!!!!!!!!!!!

(Sometimes you really do have to say
things three times!!)

Funny thing was, I didn't feel scared. It
looked at me with those shiny yellow eyes,
just for a split second, and then - whoosh!
- it was gone, back into the shadows.

And I thought: well that explains it. The whole Black Shuck thing. And I felt really happy.

I didn't bother telling the others because I knew they wouldn't believe me.

And do you know what? On the way home I also saw Father Christmas flying through the sky with his reindeer.

Ho, ho, ho!

MERRY CHRISTMAS!

Don't forget to go to www.bymistakeguide.co.uk for lots of information on how to follow in my footsteps!